I SAW HER IN MY DREAMS

I Saw Her In My Dreams

By
HUDA HAMED

Translated by
Nadine Sinno and William Taggart

Cover design by Sam Strohmeyer.
Book design by Allen Griffith of Eye 4 Design.

Library of Congress Control Number: 2022942738
ISBN: 978-1-4773-2696-1

"Did you have to collide with the world?"
—Ghassan Kanafani

TRANSLATORS' PREFACE

HUDA HAMED'S *I Saw Her in My Dreams* is a captivating novel that will both fascinate and disturb the careful and caring reader with its bold and, at times, brutal engagement with racism, particularly as directed against migrant workers in the Arab world. The novel deserves to be read and critically examined by students and scholars of Arabic literature, as well as readers worldwide, who recognize the increasing need to wrestle with issues of race and racism within and beyond the context of the Arabian Peninsula.

The novel tells three intertwined stories, told by three different narrators, Zahiyya, an Omani mother and artist who struggles with obsessive compulsive disorder and deep fear of the "Other"; Faneesh, an Ethiopian domestic worker who had to leave college in pursuit of a job in the Gulf; and Ammi Hamdan, Zahiyya's father-in-law, who spent a large part of his life in Zanzibar and was ultimately forced to abandon his African wife, Bi Soura, when the inhabitants of Zanzibar revolted against their Omani occupiers.

From the outset, the reader learns that Zahiyya is afflicted with an obsessive fear of germs, dirt, and chaos. She prefers to host friends at home because she cannot bear the thought of others "planting their filth" in her food. She does not hesitate to cut her luscious jet-black hair short upon noticing that her hair was falling out and invading her home "like snakes or cunning worms," that must be exterminated. Zahiyya acknowledges that while she is an expert at buying cleaning supplies, she is not capable of actually cleaning her home. Finding the perfect housekeeper who would transform her house into a spotless paradise—without interfering in her business or crossing boundaries—becomes Zahiyya's main challenge. She is notorious for emotionally abusing domestic workers who do not comply with her strict rules, or who dare venture out of the symbolic "square," in which she keeps them trapped. While Zahiyya is generally an unsympathetic character, the novel makes it clear that she was also a victim of abuse herself, mistreated by parents who may have loved her dearly, but who inflicted physical and verbal abuse on her in the name of chastity and reputation. Zahiyya's fear of imperfection, tendency to hurt and discriminate against those more vulnerable than herself, and recurring nightmares about a suicidal woman are directly tied to her own marginalization as a child. She is both a victim and a victimizer.

Unlike Zahiyya, Faneesh had enjoyed a rather peaceful, if impoverished, childhood in Addis Ababa. Her father's deteriorating work situation and inability to provide for his family pushes him to ask of her what many Ethiopian fathers before him had asked of their young daughters—to leave her hometown for the Gulf, where she could work as a housekeeper and send money home. Faneesh suffers her share of abuse at the hands of gang members who smuggle her into Saudi Arabia, as well as Arab employers who treat her poorly because of her black skin. Her love for reading and writing, however, lead her to write a journal documenting her story. Zahiyya stumbles upon Faneesh's diaries while searching her room, as she frantically looks for the "spell" that Faneesh may have cast on her, and which may have resulted in the transfer of the suicidal woman from Faneesh's dreams to Zahiyya's. The nightmare becomes a major motif in the novel since the suicidal woman visits Faneesh and then Zahiyya at night, terrorizing them and causing them to fear a similar fate. It is only through getting to know Faneesh as a living, breathing human being—not a robotic worker—that Zahiyya can finally begin the long process of finding salvation from her own demons.

In addition to reading Faneesh's diaries, Zahiyya reads her husband Amer's novel-in-progress. Amer's novel revolves around his father Hamdan's painful memoir, which documents his journey into and out of Zanzibar. While working with his father, Hamdan falls in love with an African woman, but he can only marry her secretly because his father cannot bear the thought of "mixing races." Shortly after Hamdan's wife Bi Soura gives birth to Amer, the locals in Zanzibar revolt against Omani rule, and a bloody war breaks out. Hamdan's father forces his son to get Amer, and they all return to Oman—leaving Bi Soura behind, robbed of her first child and husband. Hamdan never recovers from the incident, and neither does the biracial Amer, who never stopped longing for his birth mother. The ailing Hamdan prompts Amer to go back to Zanzibar, in search of Bi Soura. There, Amer fails to find his mother. Instead, he learns about his country's bloody history, the African slave market, and the fate of other Omanis who are treated as outsiders both in Oman and Zanzibar because of their mixed heritage.

I Saw Her in My Dreams is a powerful novel about interpersonal and systemic violence and the inextricability of the two in the lives of the aggressor and the aggressed. The novel explores honestly— but without sensationalizing or self-Orientalizing—the racism that has endured in the Arab Gulf. Through the relationship between

Faneesh and Zahiyya, the novel examines not only the fear of the Other, but also the possibility of healing and redemption. Without Faneesh, Zahiyya cannot confront her racism and xenophobia. Without Amer, who recognizes Faneesh's intelligence and her right to be treated with respect, Faneesh struggles to acknowledge her self-worth in Arab spaces that render her invisible. Without Zahiyya, Amer cannot survive the pain of losing his Black mother, or find the courage necessary to revisit his—and Oman's—past.

Given the current historical moment and the global fight for racial justice, this novel is bound to spark difficult but important conversations among its readers. The novel is pioneering in that it gives domestic workers in the Arab world a voice, rather than relegating them to the margins or casting them as one-dimensional characters, as is the case in many Arabic novels. Huda Hamed and we, her translators, recognize that making this novel available in English is a thorny endeavor. We realize that the novel could be "used" by some as a means of perpetuating negative stereotypes about Arabs. However, we consider it our moral imperative to translate this novel into English for several reasons. We believe that conversations about racism in the Arab world are vitally important, and that novels such as *I Saw Her in My Dreams* could play an important role in shaping these discussions. Importantly, we believe that it is crucial that the Western reader be aware that there are Arab authors who have tasked themselves with promoting regional discussions about the roots, symptoms, and manifestations of racism within the Arab world. In other words, such critiques are already happening "from the inside," as more Arab authors are articulating their concerns about the predicament of minority populations—and the fate of humanity as it relates to how we see and treat one another as breathing, feeling, thinking beings. Authors such as Hamed have taken the first steps towards voicing these painful but necessary critiques of their own societies, in part because they cherish their homelands and want them to do better with regard to their treatment of perceived "Others." Huda Hamed's novel saw publication in Arabic before the murders of George Floyd, Breonna Taylor and many others sparked worldwide protests. This attests to the author's commitment to address racial injustice in the Arab world prior to the current moment of worldwide reckoning with racial injustice. Before Hamed, activists and filmmakers in many countries in the Arab world had begun to shed light on the prevalence of human rights abuses of migrant workers, demanding more just policies and workplace conditions. These vital issues will demand much effort and attention for years to come.

Stories such as the ones exchanged among the characters in *I Saw Her in My Dreams* must be told in more languages than one. By translating this contentious novel, we hope to contribute, albeit in a very small way, to advancing discussions about race and racism in the Arab world. Despite the rise in Islamophobia and anti-Arab sentiment in the world, we consider it necessary to look inwards and identify the moments and spaces in which Arabs have engaged in mistreating the minorities among them. Fiction remains an effective way to show, not tell, where we have gone wrong and perhaps even how we might do better.

A Note on the Translation

Our translation of *Allati Ta'ud Al-Salaalim* is a result of a highly collaborative process that involved translating one chapter at a time, editing each other's work, and engaging in a series of discussions—sometimes contentious—regarding how much, or how little, we were willing to depart from the original text. Our challenges began with the title of the novel, which we initially considered translating fairly literally as "She Who Counts the Stairs" or "The Woman Who Counts the Stairs." However, we felt that both options fell short of illustrating the unusual, but effective, deployment of the feminine relative pronoun, "allati," given that "allati" is typically preceded by the noun it refers to in Arabic in the same way that the relative pronoun "who" is usually preceded by a definite noun in English. Unlike "who," however, "allati" is somehow able to not only stand on its own in Hamed's Arabic title, but also create an aura of mystery around the woman in question in a way that is both expressive and economical. Furthermore, whereas the word "salaalim" in Arabic is a plural noun that references multiple staircases, thereby painting the image of a woman repeatedly counting the steps of every stairway she climbs or descends, the noun "stairs" in English does not necessarily have the same expansive reach. After much deliberation, including a discussion with Huda Hamed, we felt that any attempt to include the English equivalents of "allati" and "Al-Salaalim" might actually risk distorting the connotation of the original Arabic title. We determined that using the two words "she who" would result in a deflated and rather "manufactured" English title, one that did not reflect the same energy, image or even meaning of the Arabic title, and the term "stairs" left us feeling equally disappointed. Quite simply, the diction, grammar, and syntax of English could not carry the weight of the Arabic in this instance.

HUDA HAMED

Our challenge with translating the novel's title is one that many Arabic-English translators have often experienced. In situations like this, translators often learn to dust themselves off after realizing that they may have just lost the first battle, but not the war. They prepare to go a different route, one that involves translating the entire novel before settling on an English title— one often inspired by the process of reading and rereading, interpreting and going back and forth between the two texts. The translators might stew, toss and turn, and even despair until the text starts speaking to them again, guiding them to an alternative translation that is faithful but not necessarily equivalent to the Arabic words themselves. In our case, the more we reread the novel, the more we realized how significant dreams were to all the main characters. Zahiyya dreamed of a mysterious woman who would visit her every time she became pregnant and predict the baby's gender. Faneesh repeatedly dreamed of a suicidal woman who had jumped off the balcony to her death in Zahiyya's house. Once Faneesh told Zahiyya about her dream, Zahiyya started having the same recurring dream—a nightmare that ultimately pushed her to confront her self-destructive and abusive behavior upon recognizing that the suicidal woman may be her alter ego, or some sort of a doppelganger whose deadly fate she might share. Aside from these literal dreams, Faneesh pursued her dream of feeding and securing a dignified living for her family despite all the pain and humiliation that she experienced as a domestic worker in the Gulf. Zahiyya fought for her own dream to study in Egypt, becoming among the first women from her village to study abroad. Meanwhile, throughout the course of the novel, we learn that Zahiyya's husband, Amer, had been dreaming of finding his African mother Bi Soura so that his father, Ammi Hamdan, may finally rest—a dream that never came true but that deeply shaped the lives of both father and son. Everyone dreamed of peace and healing from his or her respective traumas.

Crucially, the novel depicts the dream of the people of Zanzibar who longed for their independence and the painful struggles of their ancestors, some of whom had been sold in slave markets and whose dreams of freedom died with them. It also conjures up its author's and other people's dream of a more equitable Oman, one where people are not enslaved through labor or discriminated against based on their skin color, gender, or class. By calling the novel *I Saw Her in My Dreams*, we ultimately decentered the title's exclusive focus on Zahiyya—who would obsessively count the steps of the stairs—to reference the aspirations of multiple characters, including the Black domestic worker whose story we found the most intriguing. At the same time, we recognize that with every translation choice, something is gained *and* something else is lost. While we celebrate the depth and inclusivity of our new title, we still lament the loss of reference to Zahiyya's pathological compulsion. We profess and will have to live with this loss.

Aside from discussing the title with Huda Hamed and securing her approval and blessings, we involved our gracious author whenever we had questions about the original text or felt the need for her authoritative intervention, particularly as the novel is mainly set in Oman—a country that only one of us, Sinno, has visited briefly. At times, we would reach out to Huda, asking for clarification about a certain dish or a slang Omani expression, and she would promptly respond with lengthy, insightful voice messages that sometimes included images or links to more information. Needless to say, we learned a lot thanks to Huda's generosity and passion for sharing her culture. We also shared with her a sample of the translation in the earlier stages, which she diligently reviewed and discussed with friends. We thank Huda for pointing out when we did not get things right—and for encouraging us whenever we hit a milestone. This is all to say that this translation benefitted from the fruitful exchanges between Huda Hamed and ourselves, and that we strove to reach a balance concerning issues of authenticity and clarity when making translation choices. Ultimately, we were all committed to bringing this novel to life in a way that was loyal to the original Arabic language text, but that also sounded articulate and confident in English, including the times it spoke with a "foreign" accent (sometimes deliberately). To that end, we erred on the side of avoiding domestication, while also eschewing the type of stiltedness that could result from a translation that was too literal or stubborn in its insistence on replicating the original text. The balance we sought applied to both grammatical and lexical issues. For instance, we sometimes avoided replicating the tense shifts that occurred naturally in the Arabic text but that may have resulted in confusion in the English text since verb systems operate differently in Arabic and English. To elaborate, it is not uncommon for an Arab author, including Huda Hamed, to suddenly shift from past to present tense—and then circle back to the past—after establishing the general context or timeframe of a given incident. Furthermore, in Arabic, the present/imperfect tense may be used to narrate completed events, events in-progress, or even future events. While tense shifts do happen in English, such as when an author utilizes the present tense to describe a past event in an attempt to create an aura of suspense or mystery, sudden tense shifts tend to occur more frequently and exhaustively in Arabic fiction—in a way that is not always translatable without sacrificing clarity. While we generally avoided unnecessary tense shifts in the English text, we did mirror Zahiyya's use of the present tense when describing her nightmares whenever that occurred in the Arabic text, despite the fact that the events in Zahiyya's life, including her dreams, all happened in the near or far past.

We tried to capture the different registers in the novel, including its fluctuation between Modern Standard Arabic and Omani dialect by translating the dialogues and diary sections more informally than other parts of the narrative, in an effort to highlight their casual and intimate tones. We did not include any glossaries or footnotes; we trust the readers to use context clues, conduct research, and/or be at peace with feeling like an "outsider" upon encountering Arabic words with which they may not be familiar. We especially chose to keep some Arabic-language terms that were culturally significant or that revealed important information about a character's background or personality. Sometimes we embedded the meaning of Arabic words in the text itself, thereby rendering the text momentarily bilingual through the marriage of Arabic and English. We trust that our readers will enjoy encountering some words in Arabic as this should ideally give them an opportunity to imagine how the words would have been uttered by the character and to form an idea of the sound, texture, and syntax of modern standard Arabic and Omani dialect.

We agree with John Ciardi that "translation is the art of failure," and that ultimately there is no real substitute to experiencing any text in its original language. We humbly offer our translation to those who may not be able to read Arabic, but who feel a desire, or a sense of curiosity, to read an Arabic novel that has no qualms about exploring the dehumanizing impact of racial, gender, and class discrimination—as seen through the eyes of an Omani author whose work deserves much praise and further attention.

Nadine Sinno and William Taggart

I SAW HER IN MY DREAMS

ONE

I DON'T KNOW what happened to me. Between the sudden departure of Darsheen, the Sri Lankan, and the arrival of Faneesh, the Ethiopian, it felt as though I had fallen into the trap of chaos, a schadenfreude of dust. I was constantly on the run, hiding in corners that were cleaner, purer, and safer. I would catch my breath and feel a shiver run through my body. I contemplated the chaos, the particles of dust that started climbing the walls of the closets, until I was filled with anxiety.

"Who's going to clean my house in the absence of this despicable . . . ?"

My house is big. On the lower level is the women's living room, next to the men's living room, the dining room, and the formal majlis meeting room. Big windows allow light to fill the rooms every day, which brings me tremendous comfort. The wooden floors of my house groan under my feet, the creaking makes me feel ecstatic. I was happy with the choice although it's rare for Omani houses to have wooden floors. But I had insisted, especially after Chinese tiles invaded everywhere else.

I would carefully mop the spaces separating one board of wood from another, since these areas are not safe at all, while Yanni's music eased my feelings of boredom and disappointment. No one can beat me at buying cleaning supplies and concocting mixes—I even own a small notebook that includes their various names and types. I have an extraordinary ability for giving cleaning instructions. But in the midst of all of this, I shocked myself. I'm good at greedily shopping for cleaning supplies, but I'm not as good at using them.

"Damn you, Darsheen."

I love creating designs on sheilah scarfs, glass, clay pieces, and shirts. I have even painted on some of the walls of my house . . . I pay a huge fine for this love of mine. I pay from the pocket of my own emotional wellbeing because every time I find something readymade that I like, I notice some annoying or off-putting detail about it.

The situation had not been extreme or complicated, but Darsheen's absence was the final blow that made me face a world I wanted to hide from and whose existence I wanted to ignore.

On my last visit to Sharjah, I purchased different types of soft, black sheilahs so that I could decorate them with roses, branches, and other shapes whose identities I do not know well. I just fling them from my imagination to my hand.

I forcefully rubbed the rug with a small rag soaked in detergent, but the stain that my trembling hands had caused resisted me stubbornly and spread more and more. I tried hard to force it into disappearing from the new rug I'd purchased at the Chinese Market in Dubai, but it kept spreading its edges boldly and occupying additional space.

I ran toward the kitchen cabinet, full of household cleaners of all colors and shapes, and looked for the 409 Carpet Cleaner that my friend Hind said had saved her carpet from being tossed into the trash. I found a blue Clorox bottle that had "409 Carpet Cleaner" written on it. Before reading the instructions, I pressed the nozzle and then pushed both my hands on the rag in a new, serious attempt to wipe the stain from existence, but nothing seemed to work. Adding to my misery was the color fading from the brown rug. I still don't know how the thick, red-colored solution from the fabric dye had tricked me and dropped onto the rug instead of the sheilah!

I couldn't look at my rug in that wretched condition, so I called my friend Tarfa to help relieve my disappointment. After answering, Tarfa first reprimanded me as usual for giving up on Darsheen after nine years of dedicated service. Then, as if realizing that the conversation was starting to bother me, Tarfa changed the subject.

"Try using some kind of colorless soda. Or I guess you should boil some water and lemon and pour it over the stain."

I cut our conversation short. Tarfa still didn't understand that I didn't have a choice regarding Darsheen and that she was the one who destroyed her livelihood. But I wasn't going to play that broken record again. I now had two options for saving my rug. I emptied a bottle of Seven-Up over the stain, and I brought a clean rag and started rubbing. The stain started to fade, and with it, the color of the rug faded even more. I poured the hot water with lemon juice on the stain, and the sight shocked me.

"God damn you, Darsheen."

I rolled up the rug nervously, lifted it from its place, and left it close to the entrance so that Amer would understand as soon as he came back from work the necessity of taking it to the cleaner's. I washed the big brush that I had been using in the bathroom sink. I made sure that nothing remained stuck on it and poured what was left of the color solutions in the toilet. I flushed more than once and disposed of the plastic cups that I had been using.

I relaxed in the chair and imagined the possibility of things being at my beck and call. Just like that, I'd snap my fingers and the world would respond to me. My house would become suited for me, as clean and orderly as I dreamt it could be. I imagine a big mouth blowing air and removing all the dust from my house, a big mop passing over the windows and washing them in record time, a robot working to music, finishing his work in seconds by reading my thoughts, without having to open my mouth to yell or provide or repeat any advice.

Many of those who come to visit my home, either to buy sheilahs and abayas that I design and paint, or to attend the parties that my husband and I throw for our mutual friends, describe my house in the same way: "strange." Perhaps it is the open spaces I maintain between the pieces of furniture; perhaps it is the whiteness that climbs over the walls and other details; perhaps it is the curtains with bright colors; or perhaps it is the artifacts that Amer has brought me from all the countries he has visited. I arrange the artifacts on the shelves in an attractive, elegant manner that entices guests to ask about the story of each piece.

I like my house. I prefer hosting friends at my house to going out with them to restaurants because we don't know if they clean their hands and dishes as they should. We don't know whether they cover their hair so that it doesn't fall into the soup or salad they're preparing. I panic at the thought of some insect infesting their kitchen, no matter how elegant it is. My skin crawls, and I tremble. That is why I prefer inviting my friends and my husband's friends to the house even if it is "old-fashioned" according to Tarfa. So be it, I'm old-fashioned. If I'm invited to a restaurant, I don't mind having a few drops of water—from an unopened bottle—since I don't dare use glasses that have been exposed to air and hands!

Amer, Raya, and Yusuf will never forget the day we spent at a five-star hotel, laughing, singing, and eating delicious food and how things turned upside down in a second. I rushed back to the room and swore that I would not spend the night at the hotel, that I wanted to go back home. Amer tried every trick to talk me out of it, in his own kind way, but I cried bitterly as I told him about the waiter who had picked his nose with his left index finger and poured the juice with his right hand. It had happened five meters away from our table . . . but I still saw it. Amer succumbed to my wishes, despite Yusuf's and Raya's annoyance, and we went home.

I can't bear myself, so how am I supposed to bear others planting their filth in my food and drink and the place that I sleep? When I noticed that my hair was falling out in the bathroom after I had given birth to my daughter Raya, I went crazy. I went to the doctors. To the pharmacy. To the herbalists, but in vain. I felt as if the strands of my long, jet-black hair were like snakes or cunning worms climbing up the white tub and toilet, even daring to settle over my dresser. The sight killed me. That is why my decision to go to the hair salon one morning and ask the employee to give me a "boy cut" was not in vain. The Indian hairdresser was surprised. She passed her fingers through my hair and said in broken Arabic, "Your hair is beautiful, Madame. Haram, shame to cut."

I won't deny that I cried a lot when I saw myself in the mirror after I got my haircut. For the first time, I looked like my father Musabbih, my brother Mahmoud, and my cousin. The sons of the tribe all piled up in the mirror. I wasn't worried about what people would say about me because the sheilah would cover up my hair, and no one would know that I had a "boy cut."

I was worried about Amer's reaction. He would always say during our intimate moments that he loved my long, jet-black hair and my eyes. As I waited for him to come back from work, I put bright red lipstick on my lips, kohl on my eyes, and some blush on my olive skin. I parted my "boy cut" in the middle, so that my hair fell on either side of my face. I put on large hoop earrings and a white shirt with a big, purple flower that I had drawn on the left side of it. When Amer came in, I froze in place. He put his briefcase aside and contemplated me. I couldn't raise my eyes.

He approached me and ran his hand through my hair. I felt a desire to cry. I had told Amer more than once that I was going to cut my hair, but he made it clear that he didn't like the idea. I had postponed it and postponed it until the snakes appeared.

"I didn't expect the 'boy cut' to look so good on you, Zahiyya!"

I was surprised. He liked my haircut. I raised my eyes to his this time. Oh, I can't even describe how relieved I felt that moment.

Since that moment, the snakes began to disappear from my chest and from my life. They no longer occupied the bathroom or my dresser.

TWO

AMER IS DARK-skinned. His unique, beautiful brown skin made him irresistible to me when I was a student at the College of Fine Arts in Cairo. I met him during my senior year in the late eighties at the National Day ceremony that the Omani Cultural Attaché Office had organized. Amer was not a student. His visit to Egypt happened to coincide with the celebration, so his friend at the Omani Embassy invited him. I was charmed by him. I couldn't keep my eyes off him. I loved him with the speed of "love at first sight," an idea that I had never believed in.

I had put a big lock on my heart so love would not sneak into it. But I fell faster than I expected. A mutual friend introduced us to each other. During dinner, we sat on nearby chairs and talked about random things.

I learned then that he liked writing short stories. He had published his collections in different presses. He thought I would be shocked when he told me that his time was divided between his work at an oil company and between reading and writing. But that delighted me because I, too, have my own time in the company of paintings. All that Amer asks of me is an understanding for his need to write, and for the time to do it.

My grandfather hesitated a lot when Amer proposed. His family and tribe are prominent, but Amer is still the son of the African Bi Soura, and it is believed that "what is bred in the bone will come out in the flesh." It was not easy, but I stood up in my family's face and said, "Either this man, or never."

For them, I was a woman who could not be broken, for I had studied in Egypt despite some people's disdain after I earned a full scholarship from the government. I was one of the first women from my little village in al-Batina to study abroad.

"This girl is crazy and obsessive. Let's marry her off so she doesn't cause us any scandals in the courts," my father told my grandfather.

I defied my grandfather's word for the second time. I harmed my mother's reputation and disregarded my father's reluctance. I resisted the intervention of the tribe who was annoyed by the entry of a mixed lineage into its purity, and I married Amer.

On our wedding night, Amer planted his head in my neck like a clove and sobbed, and the word "ma" slipped from him unconsciously. Since that time, I have been his mother, sister, friend, and lover. I am everything in Amer's life. Amer, who did not think about looking for Bi Soura and was content with his father's stories about her. He was content with me and our babies Raya and Yusuf.

My father-in-law, Hamdan (whom I refer to as "Ammi, uncle"), has barely moved since his right leg was amputated because of diabetes. He rarely leaves the al-liwan hall that I have gotten used to seeing him in. Ammi Hamdan laughs as if the world is in his hands. His wife Jokha and her five children abbreviate their love with scarce looks and quiet smiles and stolen conversations. Ammi Hamdan won't stop repeating the same story, in different versions, every time I visit him with Amer. He just adds or omits a detail here and there, as if he is still in the spot where his amputated leg had detained him. All he can do is replay the record of memory over and over, adding his special touches and flavors every time.

Jokha, Amer's stepmother, infuriates me. She's the type of woman who does everything with infinite precision. Her house is spotless. Not one maid has entered her house throughout the forty years she has lived with Ammi Hamdan. She gives him the royal treatment. She cooks, sweeps, and cleans. She prepares the most delicious dishes. I can't resist her delicious cooking although I don't usually eat outside the home. I can't resist her tidy house that looks like no one lives in it.

It is a simple house with big empty spaces. On the bottom floor, the two salons face each other, which makes the house look bigger. The house is always filled with the fragrance of frankincense, musk, and incense. The smell radiates from the walls of the house, seats, and shelves. Jokha concocts countless recipes for incense. She mixes her potions in a special room where she hosts clients hungry for fragrances. At least that's what Amer told me. I haven't seen it with my own eyes.

Jokha prefers not to talk about her home business. She receives me with a simple smile. Her daughters and sons talk to me briefly and then leave. I sit between Ammi Hamdan and Amer so we can eat together. Jokha eats with her children in a secret place I still don't know. Maybe it is the outside kitchen or the salon on the second floor. My shyness and fear have not given me the opportunity to go up there.

Jokha comes in and then disappears. She keeps her ears with us. I feel her nervous curiosity every time Ammi Hamdan talks about his past with Bi Soura, whereas he does not care about how sensitive these kinds of conversations can be.

Jokha uses the plates of fruit as an excuse to linger. She opens and closes the containers of sweets for no clear reason. Ammi Hamdan is flush with the fever of words. His left leg stretches in front of him to compensate for the absence of the other one. The stories develop and grow, and every story goes back to his first beloved.

Bi Soura is the magnet that attracts Jokha to come and stay among us. I am now sure of that.

THEE

MY FATHER NEVER forgave me, although he had agreed to my marriage, out of fear for his reputation if his adult daughter were to go through the courts. He swore in front of my mother and siblings that he would never forgive me and that he would not enter my house. My siblings and mother supported him in the beginning since "an elder is an elder," and his word must not be broken. He was the one who led people in prayer and received religious and social enquiries from every direction. The status of my father Musabbih al-Kayumi was at the level of the venerated Sheikh Ali al-Kayumi, and he wouldn't have reached the sheikh's level if it were not for his knowledge and piety.

My mother went back on her decision. Our relationship returned to normal once I named my daughter Raya after her. I didn't expect that a matter this simple would have such an effect on her!

As soon as someone finds out that my daughter's name is Raya and my son's name is Yusuf, which are my mother's and father's names respectively, they immediately think that I gave them these names intentionally, but the real story is completely different. I gave them these names in response to a dream. Amer didn't believe in my dream when I told him about the woman who visited me and whose face I did not see. The invisible woman had put a beautiful girl into my arms and told me, "Offer prayer to the prophet and hold Raya." I offered a prayer to the prophet. I contemplated the face of the beautiful baby girl with full cheeks and woke up scared. I told Amer about the woman and the baby girl, but he laughed and didn't give the matter any attention. The heat from the woman's hand haunted me for an entire day.

I found out about my pregnancy the same month that the woman visited me. In the sixth month, I knew for sure that I was pregnant with a girl. When I told Amer about it, he said, "It's just a coincidence." Three months later, I gave birth to Raya. Amer and I didn't discuss the name. It was a done deal, maybe because of my obsession with the name "Raya," whenever I caressed my belly, asked Amer to feel her move, went for a walk, or grabbed and squeezed Amer's hand tightly during the difficult hours of labor. I got a birth certificate for Raya and put it in the box of important documents.

My mother visited me. She held Raya in her arms. She wouldn't let me bathe her or change her diapers. She did all that herself. My father did not forbid her from staying with me for forty days in a row so that she could take care of me. I told myself it was a gesture of reconciliation, but he still didn't enter my house. He didn't see his little granddaughter. My mother kept coming to my house and spoiling her granddaughter. She would sing for her the old songs that she said she used to sing to me as a child: *Bubble up coffee pot, bubble up coffee pot. Raya, you torture me with your love, you make my heart melt.*

According to my mother, the song is always the same. Only the child's name changes. Raya slept like an angel when my mother sang her this song: "Who has seen my beloved Raya? She's gone off to study. She's writing on the golden board, and the pen must be silver."

HUDA HAMED

The understanding between me and my mother didn't last for long. The dispute grew between us again, like a poisonous plant, when she interfered boldly in Raya's life and said that it was time to take her to the clinic to pierce her ears and "make her halal." These words stood at my ears like daggers. I wouldn't have even comprehended the meaning of these words if it were not for that sly gesture she made with her eyes toward that sensitive area in Raya's body.

It would be impossible for me to repeat the ugly act that my mother had carried out against me. I haven't even forgotten the face of that fat, burqa-clad woman and the trick with the dates. That swindler with sly eyes had entered our home and asked me to bring her some dates to the women's majlis. In good faith, I simply and lightheartedly brought her the dates she had asked for. She closed the door behind me and dug up her kit. Fear devoured me. I screamed and called for my mother but didn't find her. I screamed and screamed, but no one answered me. She took a rusty kit from her worn-out bundle. I closed my eyes and made a wish that I would never wake up. The pain stung me for the first time. I was seven. I still remember the trick. The closed door. The biting pain. The outburst of blood between my legs. My memory recorded that monstrous amputation. It recorded my bloodstained clothes. It recorded my tears.

The woman released me. I ran with all the blood that contaminated me. I searched for my mother's face and her smell. I wanted to throw myself into her lap and cry. But I realized it was a setup the minute I saw my mother paying the woman. Something broke in my soul in that moment. I said as much to my mother, in all honesty, nineteen years after the incident.

She smiled and laughed. "We've all been through what you have, and nothing bad happened to us. Your father has aged, and I'm still strong."

I pulled the seven-month-old Raya out of her arms and said, "Don't even try on this issue."

My mother told me about the girl sent back to her family's home by her husband because she was uncircumcised. Then she said, "We don't have to go to a cheap woman. We'll go to a clinic, where cleanliness is guaranteed."

My anger grew, and my voice got louder in my mother's face, so she got angry and stopped coming to my house except on rare occasions.

I am a woman who believes in her dreams a lot. I believed the mysterious woman who visited me twice and whose face I did not see. The invisible woman had put a beautiful girl in my arms and said to me, "Offer a prayer to the prophet and hold Raya." Then she visited me after Raya turned one and said, "Offer a prayer to the prophet and hold Yusuf." I woke up scared, and the heat from the little child was still in my lap as if he were there just a few minutes ago. I screamed. Amer woke up terrified. I told him, "Same woman, same dream. And this time she told me to offer a prayer to the prophet and hold Yusuf. I can't be pregnant. Raya is barely one." Amer held me. He said, "Meaningless dreams, my darling."

I couldn't go back to sleep. Early in the morning, I was at the pharmacy buying a pregnancy test. I went dizzy with shock when the two red lines appeared. Even Amer, who does not believe in my dreams, was baffled and unable to explain . . . Yusuf came. I didn't love him in the same way I loved Raya, but Amer's attention to him made up for my absence the first few years. With time, my feelings for Yusuf grew.

My father thought the name Yusuf was a bribe to get his approval, just like I had earned my mother's approval before. He clung to his stubbornness and fanaticism, since I was the daughter who had defied his will more than once. Yusuf carries my father's name and some of his facial features. The few times I took Yusuf with me to my parents' house, he didn't get even one glance from my father!

I rarely got together with my siblings, and when we did meet, I worried about every word, big or small. Visiting Ammi Hamdan's house was much more relaxing and reassuring than visiting my parents. With time, my visits to my parents' house shrank to three times a year—on Ramadan and the two major holidays.

FO4R

DARSHEEN, THE SRI LANKAN, stayed with our little family for nine years. She listened to orders with great attention. She executed them in absolute silence, which was what I liked about her the most. A forty-something woman, she was fat, her belly drooping, but she was as graceful as a woman in her twenties. She'd wake up at four in the morning and transform my house into something shiny. She'd return things to their places in a way that brought me comfort.

The maids before Darsheen wouldn't last in my house for more than three to seven months. They couldn't stand my watchfulness. They couldn't stand my constant instructions. They couldn't stand the rhythm of my life between guests, nightly parties, drawing, and the chaos of colors on one hand, and my strict and precise system on the other.

Boredom would soon sneak into their hearts, and they would leave. I never felt guilty. I never batted an eye. There was another line that I never allowed anyone to cross—I called this the "square." For a maid couldn't live anywhere but within a square with four sides. She was not to go beyond the tasks required of her, her own room, her bathroom, and the kitchen. I wouldn't allow the maids to have conversations with me or my children. I wouldn't allow them to know what I hid in my bags or in my bedroom. I wouldn't allow them to open anything apart from grocery bags. And what depressed them the most, according to Amer, was that they couldn't do anything without my head hanging over their shoulder.

I would keep track of every big and small detail until vindictiveness grew in their hearts. There was no room for a small mistake. No room for a fleeting slip. Every maid who entered my house realized from the very first moment that her stay wouldn't last. Amer would always tell me, "Let them breathe." But no one breathed outside the square.

I knew when a maid washed her hair, cut her fingernails, bathed, and used the bathroom. I was always ready to let them into the square so that they would not cross their boundaries. I often warned my close friends Tarfa and Hind against spoiling their maids and allowing them out of the square. Maids ran away from my house, while they stayed for a long time in my friends' houses.

I had had over twenty-five maids of different nationalities, races, and languages, but Darsheen was the only one who could understand my wishes before I even uttered them. She was able to overlook my excessive watchfulness. She kept on giving, and she liked to stay within the square. She never complained about it, and she didn't try to find out anything about me, Amer, or the kids.

She understood that I liked to see her with a head covering so her long hair wouldn't fall on the floors of my house. She understood that my heart wouldn't rejoice except when I left my bed and found the paintings, floors, walls, and souvenir gifts on the counter orderly and shiny. She knew how to make the carpet sparkle and how to clean the kitchen so I could walk on it barefoot.

She made me happy. She would arrange my closet. She knew what needed folding and what needed hanging. She'd clean the shoe cabinet and bookcases and any dirt that time may have piled up behind the wardrobes. She took care of cleaning the fans and windows. And from the time Darsheen set foot inside my house, I never saw a cockroach, and not one fly entered my house without her besieging it with her sturdy tools. All I can say is that Darsheen transformed my house into a paradise.

I would buy her expensive gifts. As soon as her travel date approached, I would negotiate with her by offering her a bonus of whatever her ticket cost, so she'd stay and not leave my house for one moment. I did this knowing that many hungry mouths awaited her in Sri Lanka. Darsheen didn't hesitate to accept my generous offer. The years grew between us as talking remained forbidden and the distance stood tall between us like concrete barriers.

I am not evil as others might think. I did allow her to go out once a month with her people. I allowed her another day a month for personal shopping, but what I would not allow at all was for her to cross the distance that stood between us.

Darsheen understood the difficult formula with the precision I needed. She was working in my house for a fee. She did not possess my house, she did not possess my secrets, she did not possess my husband's smile, she did not possess my children's time. She was selling me her time, her service, and her silence, and I was paying generously.

Amer, Raya and Yusuf disliked my exaggerated contempt for servants—as they described it. Oh, if only Darsheen transformed into a well-made Japanese machine. She would go on executing orders, and all I would have to do was plug her into a charger at the end of the night. If only this wish would one day come true so

I could get rid of my feelings of guilt every time a maid left me or another one escaped.

There are no losses bigger than losing Darsheen. That mighty woman whose face I don't remember well now. A face that was always close to the ground. I searched with great curiosity for her face in her identification papers after her departure. But even in the pictures, her head was bowed, her headdress nearly covering her face. I could barely tell that she had eyes.

Darsheen tolerated my angry outbursts. She tolerated my loud voice. She tolerated my migraines and my angst and, with the skill of a sponge, she absorbed me, her head bowed. It was as though bearing my fluctuating mood and outbursts counted among her other duties—cleaning, tidying up, and doing laundry—before toddling into the square like a chicken toddles into her master's coop.

I saw her with my own eyes chopping onions without any gloves on. She raised her head as I cursed her. She looked me in the eye for the first time in nine years, for so long that I lowered my head. I trembled as she said to me in her broken Arabic, "Madame . . . khalas, it's over."

After the ninth year, her voice emerged deep and forceful like the whirlwind of a tornado. It was during the time I wanted to negotiate with her over presents and the cost of the ticket and a new contract. She refused my blessing. She refused my lucrative offer. She rushed to her room. I told myself that Darsheen would calm down and things would go back to normal—that she would accept the gifts and ticket money in order to silence the hungry mouths that awaited her, go back to finish the cleaning spree she loved, rub the sofa in the living room with a wet rag, run the rag over the folds of my curtains, water Amer's trees, and pull out the weeds.

Darsheen came downstairs, dragging her bag. She didn't talk to me. She walked past me as if she hadn't seen me. Like I used to walk past her. She stood in front of Amer with her head up, to the point that I thought she had grown taller.

"Boss, I want to go. My contract khalas, done. I go, not come back."

My heart stopped when she said "go, not come back." I went up to my room. I cried like a baby. No, I wasn't going to talk to her. I wasn't going to ask her to stay. I wasn't going to tell her that I'm only good at buying cleaning supplies and giving orders. Who was she to do that to me? Who did she think she was?

How had she opened the square and left? How had I entered the damn square to cry alone?

Darsheen had opened the door of the square with her hand and left at the time she wanted, at the time that "she could not stand me any longer," as Amer, who bought her the ticket, commented. He gave her an end of service reward, and the whole thing was over in less than three days.

Darsheen left my house, and feelings of disgust haunted me. Dirty dishes haunted me. My paint, sheilahs, abayas and the guests I'd forbidden from visiting haunted me. Darsheen left, and I closed the curtains so that I wouldn't look at the windows as dust hugged them hungrily. The morning shine and the smell of frankincense in the morning and night left with her. Gone were the noises of friends, their nightly mayhem, and the chaos that Darsheen would wave away with her magic wand, transforming it in the blink of an eye into a paradise that I wanted to spend the rest of my life in.

FI5VE

NO ONE BELIEVES that after twenty-one years of marriage to Amer, our hearts still beat with as much love, desire, and yearning, as they did the first time we met. During our parties, my friend Hind would laugh and say, "Zahiyya beautifies her marital life just like she beautifies sheilahs, shells, and walls."

Tarfa would nudge me on the shoulders. "Offer prayer to the prophet, folks, against anyone who might give them the evil eye."

We'd offer a prayer to the prophet, and infectious laughter would break out among us. Rashed, the great businessman and Hind's husband, would stress that we should always be discreet about our private affairs and joys, but I don't understand this logic! Khaled, Tarfa's husband, would point out that those who talk about their happiness are given strange names, "boastful, pompous . . . "

Amer annoyed me, or rather destroyed me, with one thing that I put up with silently. It might seem naïve, but it was a killer. It would get on my nerves, electrocuting me. I had never been able to tell him that I hated his garden so much, even though it beautified my house. It bothered me when it got too excessive. It became a haven for insects and snakes. It bothered me every time it stained my children's clothes, and every time bleach failed to absorb the stains. I remember how loudly we'd screamed when a snake snuck into the guest bedroom on a hot day to cool off, but my anger didn't change anything. "A snake snuck in and met its end, and it's over," Amer had said, and the three of them continued to dirty my house.

Beautiful cactuses grow in my backyard. A fig tree. Succulent "Al-Khalas," palms that a friend brought me from Ibri. Jasmine and Yas at the gate's entrance. Our bedroom window overlooks a lily patch and a lemon tree that bears abundant fruit.

Amer spends hours in the garden cutting, trimming, and watering. He transformed the backyard into a paradise in a short period of time. Raya and Yusuf also caught the gardening bug. They developed a relationship with water and mud. They played and got dirty. With time, they learned a lot of things about trees, proper watering needs, and about which plants need to stay outdoors and which ones must share with us our air-conditioned rooms. About plants that bear fruit, and those that flower.

Amer's plants would distract him from human beings. From forming friendships. He was content with me and the children and the garden. More than once, I considered pulling out his trees when he was gone at the oil company where he works as an engineer. But I didn't. Maybe because he doesn't ask much of me. Just to leave him this small space where he can breathe.

6

I SLOWLY WALKED up to my house on day twenty-one of Darsheen's absence. I climbed the stairs to my room like someone who wanted to avoid everything. I climbed the stairs, thinking. Where did all that dust come from when my house had been locked the entire time? How did it sneak in to spite me like that? How did it enter in between the tightly stacked books in the bookshelf that I had arranged with outstanding care?

Amer's books on politics and economics, which he brings with him from his long travels, sit on the top shelves, followed by Yusuf's history and philosophy books, and then Raya's books of poetry, short stories, and novels. There aren't any books that belong to me. I am more interested in fashion magazines than anything else. I arrange those in a closet where hands and dust cannot reach them. On one side of the bookshelf, I keep a large number of music CDs that I like to listen to when Amer is working at the oil company or traveling and while Raya and Yusuf are away studying in Australia.

I climbed the stairs, thinking about the way the brown cabinet looked, the one between the kitchen and the living room, where souvenir pieces from all the countries I have visited with my family are lined up. Oh, God. I couldn't look at it in that moment. I wished I could bypass its existence in my house. I didn't know Darsheen's secret to making my house so clean, just as I liked it. If only she hadn't given me that look. If only she had bowed her head and not raised it in my face during that moment of anger. Who knows, maybe it would have been possible for me to forgive her.

I paused as I climbed the stairs. I raised my head. I was shocked by the paintings that seemed to frown at me on the white wall. It had been three weeks since anyone had dusted them. I climbed and climbed without looking at anything. I entered my room, which I keep impeccably clean.

I took off my abaya. I put it on the stand. I went into the bathroom that I always keep dry even from the smallest droplets of water. I washed my face well with a face wash for removing makeup. I brushed and flossed my teeth. I put sanitizer on my hands. I wore my pink nightgown. I pulled my short hair back with an elastic band. I wiped the sink and toilet seat with a rag. I put everything back in its place. I went out to find Amer lying down on the side of the bed holding a book he had been reading for over a week. I buried my head in his chest.

Amer's phone went off. I guessed from his responses that he was talking to the "maids' office." I also understood that the new maid wasn't going to arrive and that the chaos was going to eat at me for a longer period of time.

Amer ended the phone call saying, "The office is stalling. That's it. I've decided. We'll go to the al-Ain office and get a maid."

SE7EN

AMER AND I stepped out of the car. We entered the office for the recruitment of foreign domestic workers in al-Ain. A Filipina woman in her forties received us with a wide smile. She was elegant despite being short and thin. We sat across from her.

She asked us about our aspirations. "Do you want someone who's Indian, Sri Lankan, Indonesian, Filipina, or Ethiopian? Do you want someone who knows how to cook? Take care of the children? Educated? Uneducated? Someone who has worked in the Gulf before or not?"

There were so many questions. Amer and I were stunned. We just sat there with no answers. The Filipina woman—who seemed to run the office—gestured with her hand, and six workers of different nationalities approached us.

"You can choose," the Filipina woman said.

The whole thing was like a big slap in the face. Each one of them spoke politely about what distinguished her, gently winking at me to pick her. I was still in shock and couldn't decide on anything.

The Filipina woman led me to the "store"—as she referred to it—on the bottom floor. I had thought that I didn't have a choice beyond the six young women on the upper floor, but I was surprised to find scores of workers. They were all gathered together in one place. My heart raced. I was shocked by the sight. A few had secured some chairs to sit on, while others sat on their suitcases. Another group was lying on the floor, in a deep sleep. Different colors, shapes, nationalities, and languages. One tried to lure me with her broken Arabic, while another promised to take care of my children. A third one swore that she was good at everything. Cooking and cleaning. A fourth one haggled with me over her salary. I was struck with dizziness and panic by what I had seen.

Amer was waiting for me on the upper floor. I didn't know where I had descended to. How would one categorize this place? I told myself, "My house and my tight square are more humane than this wretched place." They kept chasing me, as I stood confused, unable to make a decision. I looked for a face that looked like Darsheen's, but her features slipped away from me.

Oh my God, if only I could go back in time for a little bit. I would overlook her chopping the onions without gloves. I would tell her not to do that again, but I wouldn't curse her.

"Damn you, Darsheen. Damn."

I couldn't stand their sticky bodies. I couldn't stand their jostling around me or the dirty spray that dashed out of their mouths toward my face. I had dealt with many nationalities. I had tried Filipinas, Indonesians, and Sri Lankans. I never dared to go near Indians or Ethiopians for fear of the lack of cleanliness that they were usually known for. Amer would call that "racism."

I didn't feel drawn to any of them. But what did it mean for me to have come all this way only to return empty-handed? I gave up and sat in an empty chair. I couldn't think of another solution as another client in an embroidered abaya strutted among them. Once again, they surrounded the woman, and the series of lucrative offers started all over again.

I sat next to a woman. I quickly figured out that she must be of African ethnicity because of her color, height, nose, and eyes.

She didn't move from her place. She didn't fight to showcase her distinctive characteristics like her peers of other nationalities had done. I shot her an inquisitive look. She seemed clean, neat, and not sweaty. Her nails were clipped. Her toenails were tidy. Her hair was covered properly with a short scarf. She seemed young, capable of working and following instructions.

I thought to myself that change might be beneficial. Who knows? Maybe an Ethiopian would be more tolerant of my demands and strict conditions. I turned to her again while she pretended to be busy looking in a different direction. I asked her to tell me about herself, and she surprised me with her English:

"My name is Faneesh. I am from Ethiopia, I worked in Saudi Arabia for five years and in Dubai for less than a year. I can cook, wash clothes, and iron. I also have experience cleaning and taking care of babies."

"I don't have babies. But the issue of cleanliness is very important to me."

"Don't worry ma'am. I was trained at the hands of a Filipina maid."

I had a pretty good feeling about her, but I became worried as soon as she raised her head and said, "But ma'am."

I nodded, gave her an opportunity to speak.

She asked, "Does it matter to you that I pray?"

Dumbfounded, I answered her, "Of course it doesn't matter to me. I mean, that's your private relationship with God, and I'd never interfere with it."

We were both silent, and then I interjected. "Speaking of prayer, what's your religion?"

"I am Christian. I converted to Islam in Saudi Arabia."

I was very surprised by the way she said that sentence, but it wasn't very important. She seemed like soft dough, ready to be shaped, and I was brilliant at that.

I went upstairs with her to the director's office. I asked her to complete Faneesh's paperwork as soon as possible. Amer was amazed. He gulped as he saw me pointing to an African girl.

I winked at him and said, "Maybe change will bring about good results, Amer."

EIGHT

I PREPARED FANEESH'S paperwork and her exit visa from the United Arab Emirates to Oman. I couldn't bear not knowing the details of her converting to Islam. I watched her in the front mirror of the car. Faneesh watched the buildings and streets. She held her head up high. As soon as I would talk to her, she would look me straight in the eye, contrary to Darsheen whose head was always lowered. Faneesh spoke with a certain level of confidence. Her English, mixed with Arabic, betrayed the fact that she had had some education. I worried about taking initiative by asking questions and talking to her because first encounters with maids determine the pattern of the relationship later. I worried about breaking the barriers between us, making the mission of leading her into the square later on harder. I wanted to kill the long commute with some kind of conversation, but my complicated calculations kept gnawing at me. Smoothly and lightly, Amer turned down the music, raised his head, and started talking to Faneesh.

"Faneesh, why don't you tell us a little bit about yourself?"

Faneesh was sitting right behind me. I moved my head so I could watch her in the side mirror.

"My story is long, boss. I don't think it's important."

Did she have other hidden surprises—aside from the confident way she sat, the straightness of her back against the seat like a lady, and her ability to speak clearly with her head up? The way she moved her hands and smiled at us, as if she were about to start a friendship with us? Did she have other surprises, aside from the look she directed at my side mirror at times and the front mirror at others? What else?

"I worked at three houses, two in Saudi and one in Dubai."

"Aha. Good. Tell us about yourself and about Ethiopia, your education, for example, or your family."

Faneesh was enjoying Amer's persistence, his eagerness to learn more about her. His attitude frustrated me. His friendliness. I felt a burning sensation in my stomach. I felt nauseated as Faneesh continued to speak with confidence.

"I was raised in the coffee fields in Addis Ababa. My father was waiting for a son for his first child, someone who could help him on the coffee farm, but here I was, a girl. My father loved me so much. But I loved going to school more. He managed to secure my school fees and supplies when he sensed my passion for knowledge. I used to walk a long distance to get to my school. My father was down on his luck, and his income declined, so he kept me at home after elementary school. He told me that my brother Jerma's education was more important than mine. I felt depressed at the time."

Amer raised his head, gestured for her to keep going. Faneesh's face regained its liveliness. Her appetite for talking grew, as Amer, in his usual way, broke the barriers that I was building. My breathing grew louder as Faneesh spoke.

"Things weren't that wretched, sir. I started nibbling at the books that were available to me. I would write in the margins of my notebooks so I wouldn't forget what I learned. Jerma would toss his stuff. He'd skip or run away from school sometimes. I peeked in his books and dared to do his homework."

Faneesh laughed as if she was about to become our friend, as if we were suddenly at the same level, no difference between us. As if we'd known each other for decades or had been raised together. Oh, Amer, I hate you so much right now. How fragile and gullible you are! Faneesh continued her story.

"My brother Jerma conspired with me, sir. He was getting perfect grades, and I was getting regular practice by doing his homework."

Amer might as well have been clapping for her. His heart swelled and fluttered like a child who had gotten a toy.

"Good choice, Faneesh."

"My friend Zanash, who was a few years older than me, also deserves a lot of credit. Zanash works with UNICEF, which advocates for women's education. She would lend me some English-language books that were very hard for me to read at first. But I persisted at learning, and I'd go to her sometimes and ask her questions. I'd come back more excited to read during the little free time I had. You know what, sir? When my father noticed my interest in reading and learning, while Jerma was busy messing around, he sent me back to school, on the condition that I'd help him in the fields during my free time. I divided my time between the coffee farm and school. Life smiled at me, and so I went to college. I completed my first year in the College of Arts, in the English department."

I was surprised by Faneesh's story. Was it possible that she had gone to college and then ended up this way, as a maid in my house? It's all your fault, Amer. You give maids the opportunity to lie every chance they can! I am not a stranger when it comes to the lies of maids. I have had my taste of them. Amer went back to asking her questions, with even more interest this time.

"You went to college, Faneesh? Aha. I had a feeling. Your way of speaking . . . and your English is good. And then what? What happened to this beautiful life?"

Faneesh's tone of voice changed a little. She seemed to enjoy the golden opportunity to weave more stories. Amer believed her, as if she had escaped from the books he read regularly. He unearthed stories with her. It was as if he was about to take her—in flesh and blood—into the novel that he'd been writing for years and that I hadn't been able to read or know anything about. He tells me that writing is an intimate thing, something that resembles a fetus in the womb. He should not be seen or taken into the light until he has completely developed and is ready for natural birth. Frankly, I don't know when his novel will be ready for its birth. He has been writing it since elementary school according to what Ammi Hamdan has told me. He has been writing down all the stories he hears from his father about Zanzibar and about his mother Bi Soura. He saves everything in a white, translucent folder. Numerous blue notebooks and papers. He is rewriting the novel on his laptop. Raya, Yusuf, and I are not permitted to look inside that white folder. When it's time to clean the office, Amer hides the folder away from prying eyes until the annoying business of cleaning the office is over, as he puts it. Amer has shared with us other stories that he has written and published by *al-Intishar al-Arabi*, and we attended his last book-signing event at the book fair in Muscat. I remember very well when the journalist Suleiman al-Maamary asked him during his show "The Cultural Scene," about his next book. He said, "It's going to be a novel." It's been three years since the publication of his last short story collection,

Joy Ululates. For three years, he has been working two hours a day, but the time for the birth of his novel has not come yet! Faneesh resumed talking.

"The hungry mouths in my family multiplied. Every couple of years, my mother would give birth to a brother or sister. My father, who was a laborer in the coffee fields, had no choice but to broach this subject with me."

Faneesh stopped talking. I spied on her from behind my sunglasses. She was taking a breath, or maybe she was cooking up a lie.

"My father told me, 'I need your help, Faneesh.' I didn't know what kind of help my father would want from his eldest daughter. My mother started sobbing nonstop as she wrapped her arms around my neck from behind my seat. I understood. The story had played out repeatedly in our neighbors' houses. A father, choked by words. A mother crying bitterly. And a daughter, leaving for work in the Gulf. My father said in a worried voice, 'It's need, Faneesh. It's need that is pushing me to ask you for this.'"

Her dirty trick worked on Amer. His voice changed. He seemed empathetic to her just like he empathized with the characters he creates.

"Did your father force you to travel?"

Faneesh lowered her head and then raised it back up.

"My father cut corners personally so I could study. He saved every Birr he made for my sake. The mouths around him would widen every day, and his back became hunched. I had to return the favor, sir."

I was not part of their game. I listened to them, amazed by the girl's lies and by Amer's fragile heart.

Amer asked, "What was it like working in Saudi Arabia? And, by the way, what's the story about you converting to Islam?"

I felt great rage as Amer transformed the maid into a woman who was about to join the family as one of its members. I did not care about her, but Amer was giving her voice importance. I shot him a reprimanding look. But he didn't notice me. Maybe he ignored me.

Amer parked the car near a gas station in the district of Sohar. He looked at me and asked, "Where are we going to have lunch?" I suggested having lunch at Pizza Hut. He agreed. Amer knew I wouldn't dare eat anything but a green salad. I thought about how the three of us were going to sit at the same table. Faneesh found the solution. She sat at a table that was two tables away from us, without anyone asking her to do so. Good job Faneesh. There were things in our relationship that I could fix as soon as we got home. Amer came back carrying salads and two pizza boxes. Then he gestured to Faneesh.

"Faneesh, come sit with us. We'll hear the rest of your story while we eat."

At that moment, I felt a serious desire to turn the table over in Amer's face. I hinted to him with my eyes that I didn't approve. Faneesh caught that before Amer did.

"Sir, it's OK. I am comfortable sitting at this table by myself."

I pretended I was going to the restroom. Amer followed me. He said, laughing, "What's going on, Zahiyya? Are you seriously jealous? You know she's Raya's age, right?"

I raised my hand and voice at the same time. "I'm jealous of this filthy liar? Look what you've done, Amer. First you listen to her stories, and then you ask her to eat with us."

Amer took a deep breath. He wrapped his arms around me with extreme tenderness. Then he threw a bomb in my face.

"Your whole life, you've been treating maids like insects under your feet. And I've told you, Zahiyya, it doesn't work."

I noticed people looking at us. They let their food get cold so they could watch us. I was terrified when Amer left me. I saw him join Faneesh at her table. I took a deep breath. I calmed down a bit. I came back and sat with them as if nothing had happened. I took the salad plate. I stirred the vegetables with a fork to ensure that they were properly washed. I put the fork in my mouth. The three of us stopped talking, and Amer didn't ask any more questions. Faneesh hid her eyes away from me.

I woke up from my sleep. I sat on my bed. Amer had left for work. I hugged the pillow as bitter depression rose to my throat. I thought, was it not a serious transgression for me to choose an Ethiopian after being so blessed by the cleanliness of Filipinas, Indonesians, and Sri Lankans? Was it not a transgression, Amer giving her all that space to talk? I expelled the bad thoughts out of my mind. I enjoyed a hot bath. Shampoo dripped down my face, over my closed eyes. I thought, can you, Faneesh, be like air, and remain quiet? Can you be like electricity, so that I might feel your presence but not see you? Can I wake up to find my house full of life . . . the windows all shiny and open to sunlight, the smell of incense radiating from the downstairs rooms to my room upstairs? Can I walk around barefoot on the wooden floors without feeling disgusted and nauseated? Can you give me back my energy and lightness, so that I can draw again on the black sheilahs and abayas with loud colors, without suffering from the urge to look at the chaos? Do that for me, and I will spoil you with a good salary, with gifts that you may have never even dreamed of. Clean and sweep and cut the vegetables into equal-sized pieces. Put things in their exact place as if they had not been touched yet, as if hands had never touched them before, for this makes me feel reassured, Faneesh. Cover your hands well with gloves while you are washing the bathrooms and be sure to wear the other set of gloves designated for the kitchen. And before doing anything, make sure that not one stray hair of yours leaves your head covering. Do not allow your footsteps to find their way to my ears when I'm busy drawing and painting. Wear soft slippers whose sound cannot be heard or felt. Do that, Faneesh, for these things are what will enable you to stay in my house longer.

I put on my clothes and prepared myself for a long talk with Faneesh. I went down the stairs leading to the living rooms. My soul gasped with great surprise. It was as if I wasn't in my house, the house that I had been running through a couple of days ago with my eyes closed so that I wouldn't have to face things. Oh my God! It was as if Darsheen had suddenly come back. Was it a dream or reality? Faneesh leapt in front of me wearing an elegant uniform from the collection I had given her upon her arrival, along with some clean undergarments, gloves, and head coverings. Faneesh smiled, bowed her head, and greeted me. I smiled at her, full of surprise. When had she been able to do all that, this daughter of a demon?

I stood with my feet on the shiny floor. The smell of Detol emanating from the bathrooms tickled my nose. I walked barefoot on the kitchen floor for the first time since Darsheen's departure. Everything was in its place. Faneesh had not asked me about anything. It was as if she knew where things belonged with infinite precision. She knew where the cleaning supplies were and what each of them was used for. It was as if she'd been living in this house all along. She had arranged my coloring tools. She had shaken out the rugs and put them aside. She had cleaned the fans. She had opened the windows and allowed light to sneak into the living room. I was surprised by the kitchen cabinets. She had lined the drawers with plastic and reorganized the kitchenware in a way that delighted me.

This demon, where had she come from?

I wanted to applaud. I wanted to tell her, "You understand what I want even before I speak. You are a miracle maker." But no. I wasn't going to do that because she'd escape from the square that I was trying to lead her into. She stood in front me. She was slightly taller than me, her body slim and proportional. I noticed her quick movement, her perfect work. She didn't miss any details. It was as if my morning wish, under the hot water and shampoo in the shower, had come true. It was as if I had rubbed the magic lantern, and the genie had come out to make my little wish come true with a blow over Faneesh's head.

She asked me if I was going to have my breakfast then. I found myself answering her firmly, "You have no business preparing food. Got it? I am the only one here who prepares food."

Her color changed. Her smile shrank. I barely noticed her nod as she retreated from me to continue cleaning. I prepared milk tea with saffron this time. It is the tea of good moods and postponed celebrations. I put the tea on a tray, along with some bread, cheese, and olives. I grabbed my phone and talked to Raya and Yusuf. I told them the news about Faneesh's arrival. I told them that it looked like that she was going to outperform Darsheen. They were happy for me, but at the end of the phone call, Raya added, "Ma . . . take it easy on her."

I resented that expression, which Amer and the kids always used. No, I wasn't going to "take it easy" on her. She had to stay in her designated area so I wouldn't oppress or judge her. I alerted Faneesh to the importance of not asking questions. She must only execute orders. I alerted her to the importance of not chatting with my guests. Nothing more than a passing greeting.

"I will call you whatever name you like. I don't have any problem with anything related to the hijab or prayer—that's your personal choice. But covering your hair is important, not for religious reasons, but so I don't shudder every time your hair falls into my food or on my floor. You will have a vacation twice a month, once to buy your own things and once to meet with your acquaintances or, if you wish, visit the church. What matters to me are cleanliness and good intentions."

That was the last thing I said in preparation for my attempt to walk her into the square. Just so she wouldn't think that the stories she told Amer were going to get her any empathy from me.

Faneesh withdrew with the lightness of a feather. I didn't hear her footsteps, thanks to the cotton slippers she wore. I didn't hear her voice or the sound of the cleaning tools. Everything proceeded according to the rules I had established. Oh, maids! Like a soft dough, ready to be shaped. We just have to say with courage what we want from them and not do away with intimidation and enticement. What's even more important than any of this is maintaining the distance between us and them as if they are not there. As if we don't see them.

I went into the kitchen and started preparing a delicious meal for Amer. Faneesh chopped up the vegetables in small, equal-sized pieces. She wore gloves the entire time and covered her hair with a short hijab. She rinsed any container that I used as I worked. Throughout our stay in the kitchen, Faneesh didn't open her mouth. She didn't say anything. Oh, how much I love this human "robot." I knew not to express my admiration for what she was doing. It was part of her duties, for which she was going to receive a fee at the end of every month. Amer arrived at the right time. I put the delicious salads and chicken biryani on the table. Amer couldn't control himself when he entered the house.

"The house is full of life again, finally!"

I put my hand over his mouth. I asked him to be quiet so she wouldn't get a big head and we'd lose control of the situation. Amer stopped talking. We sat down to eat, and we talked about many things, as if my heart had come to life again. I was fun, childlike, mischievous, and playful. I know very well that Amer loves to see me sparkle, but that he gets upset when depression eats at me, and I become silent and dim.

Faneesh hid somewhere. I did not feel her eyes spying on us or her ears eavesdropping on our conversation. Her body stopped moving. Oh! She seemed trained and ready to me. There was no need for more yelling or the repetition of advice and orders.

N**9**E

"I WONDER WHO these wide, narrow, almond eyes belong to. Who do these big lips, these tiny lips like pistachios, belong to? Where does this short, long, flat nose come from? From whom do you take this fair, olive, black skin? Where does this skinniness, this chubbiness come from? Who'd you inherit your joyful mood from? Your bad mood? Whose silence, whose mischief, whose laughter do you take after? Whose—?" That's how questions grow. As soon as a new baby comes into the world. The questions grow until every one of us has accounted for a piece of the little visitor. It is as if our opportunity for immortality is made possible by the presence of someone who resembles us, someone who snatches one of our features.

Amer has his mother's dark skin color, her soaring height, her thin fingers. His body falls between her voluptuous figure and his father's excessive skinniness. He has his mother's thick, curly hair, that he sometimes grows shoulder-length or shaves off completely, which makes him look like one of those rappers, as Raya says jokingly. He has his father's straight Arab nose, his small lips, and his yearning heart. He has his father's laugh, his small, tightly packed teeth. He has their story—that's what Ammi Hamdan says. Amer didn't have a problem with having Arab features but extremely dark skin. He didn't even have a problem with the nickname "son of Bi Soura, the Swahili woman" that his grandfather had given him and that had stuck with him. He was at peace with himself even though some people used his background as a means to spite him. Amer came to love his mother Bi Soura very much from Hamdan's stories, from the pictures he drew in his head every day and that he painted in order to burnish his memories of her—until he started to see her and hear her laughter in the house. Amer was not breastfed by his mother except for one time, right after he was born. His first and last day in East Africa. Then his grandfather kidnapped him from his mother's bosom before she could take a good look at him, before she could memorize his features, before she could sing to him. The only thing he had from her was the leso garment that she'd wrapped around him to protect his delicate body. Ammi Hamdan had saved that piece of leso in a special trunk where he keeps his most valuable belongings. He let Amer look at it once only upon Amer's insistence.

Amer likes to tell me stories about making paper and cardboard planes in his childhood, planes that he flew in the direction of Zanzibar, hoping they would reach his mother. Defective planes that hovered a little and then fell in the backyard. They bumped into the wall. They bumped into the palm trees. They didn't last long. Ammi Hamdan would untangle the kites that Amer had colored and under whose wings he'd written the message "to be delivered to my mother, Bi Soura." Zanzibar remained a legendary place of adventure that Amer searched for in books, questions, and the stories of returning visitors, but he didn't dare go. He had traveled to many countries, but he wouldn't go near that area. Every time I'd ask him about it, he'd say, "not now." Ammi Hamdan returned from Zanzibar to Nizwa during the British coup. There, he married his cousin Jokha. With her, he had Amer's five half brothers and sisters—Amer's white siblings, the ones with bright red cheeks and noses straight as daggers. Jokha trained him to refer to her as "Ma Jokha." Her delay in getting pregnant for over four years from the time she got married strengthened her relationship with Amer. After giving birth to her own children, she taught Amer's siblings to respect him as he was their eldest brother, their "backbone."

Amer didn't grow up with an inferiority complex as some people like to think. He was loved by his family and was outstanding in his studies. He loved his family. He loved his mother Jokha and his father Hamdan with his stories. He loved his secret past. He studied engineering and joined an oil company that paid a good salary. If I spoil him for an hour, he spoils me for many more. His yearning for his mother's face burns in his heart, so he tucks his head into my bosom. I run my delicate fingers through his hair and massage his scalp until he gets drowsy and falls asleep. I see him curled up like a fetus at the edge of the bed, so I pull him close again. Yusuf and Raya grew up quickly. But Amer never grew up. He kept getting younger and younger every day. He needs me more now. I am ecstatic with happiness. I like this game. It's as if Amer is threatened by loss for the second time, as if he might come home one day and discover that he doesn't have a wife and kids. That we're just a bubble that he had created in his mind. He has opened up to me honestly about his fears. He squeezes himself to my chest during those drowsy moments. I run my fingers over his body. I contain him. He wonders, "What if my father Hamdan and his stories disappear from my life? What if Jokha and my siblings disappear? What if you were a lie, Zahiyya? What if Yusuf and Raya were just mirages?" I shower him with kisses. I don't take my hands off him. I let him talk and talk. I don't know who falls asleep before the other. But we wake up exactly as we were, clinging to each other, with stories that have not been completed between us. Amer says he envies me because my obsessions float to the surface. A frown, a loud voice, intense crying, and then it's all over. I don't let things accumulate. I settle all my scores from the get-go. I cry on his shoulder in the movie theatre. I cry like a little girl if my dress gets dirty, but I recover quickly. Amer always asks me, "Is that why women live longer than men? They empty their sadness from the get-go. They settle their scores from the get-go. Women spill secrets and tears, while we men hoard them. I'm almost certain that's why their mischievous lives are prolonged while ours are shortened."

Amer expressed to me his desire to visit Ammi Hamdan. His health was getting worse. Amer is attached to his father and to his father's stories like someone attached to a secret rope. I know how much worry eats him up every time he hears that his father's health is getting worse. I understand Amer. I understand his eagerness. I understand his closeness to his father. Ammi Hamdan, the man who has blessed every step that Amer has taken in life, while my family would trip me time after time. I would get back up and start running and running. They thought about cutting off my feet so I would stop moving completely, so I closed my eyes and ran, whereas Ammi Hamdan applauds every step that Amer takes.

Ammi Hamdan wept. How cruel that moment was. The tears of children are less painful than those of an elderly man. Amer patted his shoulders as he held back his own tears. Jokha explained to us that his health had deteriorated in the past few days. Amer held his father's hand firmly as tears trickled down his face. He choked on his words to the point that we couldn't understand what he was saying. His five children went in and out of the room and seemed worried. Ammi Hamdan calmed down a little. He started singing in Swahili, a language that we don't know. Amer understands a few words that his father had taught him as a child. He had also learned some words from his Swahili coworkers at the Omani oil company.

What's happening to you, Ammi Hamdan, during this critical time? Why do you remember, in these moments of sickness and exhaustion, a lover with whom you only spent a few years, while forgetting about Jokha—the woman who has spent an entire lifetime with you, in sweetness and in bitterness? I felt her nervousness every time Ammi took a trip down memory lane to the first woman he loved. I saw her anger and her fear for him at the same time. Jokha is an invisible woman because she was never Ammi Hamdan's choice. He closed his eyes after laying them on Bi Soura, and he never opened them again. How many times did he say in front of Amer and me, and even in front of Jokha herself, "I didn't want *her*"? How many times did he drive his words like a spear into her heart? Through it all, she remained calm and content, as if this was her fate and she had to accept it.

Ammi Hamdan pulled Amer to his chest; he searched for Bi Soura's smell in him. Meanwhile, Amer wrapped his arms around Hamdan so he could hold his father's frailty—a sight that almost drove me to tears. I left the gloomy room and went outside where guests who were relatives of Ammi Hamdan and Jokha had gathered. Oh goodness, how stifled I felt amidst all those bodies. How uncomfortable I felt.

One of Jokha's female friends said to a woman sitting beside her, "What if his first wife had cast a spell on him?"

HUDA HAMED

The other woman responded, "An African woman would definitely do that."

The women swallowed their tongues as soon as Jokha passed in front of them with a pot of coffee and a plate of dates. I spent a long time in silence waiting for Amer. I exchanged some looks and a few smiles with the visitors. I watched those whose pain gnawed at them over Ammi Hamdan's situation and those who came just to broadcast stories. Amer came out suddenly, and I followed him. His face was red. His eyes were red. He entered the kitchen, so I stood directly behind him. He planted some money in Jokha's hand.

"You'll need the money. There's plenty of guests, Ma Jokha."

Jokha tucked the money into her pocket, gratitude clearly showing on her face. She asked us to stay for dinner, but Amer apologized. As if he'd just remembered something, he added, "Ma Jokha, my father needs medical treatment. I am planning a trip for him."

The color drained from Jokha's face, and she suddenly looked like a mummy.

"Don't worry. It's just for good measure. Nothing more. But I will travel by myself and check out the situation first."

Jokha begged Amer to take her with him, but he gently declined, under the pretext that the children needed someone to take care of them. She stopped talking and withdrew to attend to new guests who had rang the doorbell.

Amer and I left. We got in the car. I, too, had questions about this sudden trip. We had gotten used to Ammi Hamdan's frequent bouts of illness, his diabetes at times and depression at others, so what was different this time around? I waited for Amer to open his mouth and say something, anything.

He shocked me when he said, "Zahiyya, I deceived my mother Jokha. My father and I have been planning to go to Zanzibar to search for my mother Bi Soura. But since my father is not feeling well, I'm going by myself. If I find her, I'll bring my father to see her."

I gasped. Questions ate me up. I found myself turning with my entire body to look at him, as he was about to start driving. Was what you were saying even possible, Amer? After all these years, what will you go looking for exactly, and how and where and when?

My questions remained hanging in the air.

10

AMER HUGGED ME tight. I stroked his back gently with my hands. His suitcase was a few steps away from us. Amer had traveled a lot, but this time he seemed extremely emotional, scared, nervous, sad, happy. He pushed a folder into my hands:

"Zahiyya. I printed for you a copy of the novel I've been writing since I was a child. Or rather it's my father Hamdan's life story."

"You're finally done writing it?"

"No, I haven't finished it. I might figure out a good ending for it in Tanzania."

I was surprised. These papers almost destroyed our relationship ten years ago. Amer used to keep them in a secret place in the study. Curious, I had flipped through the pages, under the pretext that I was ensuring the office was clean, and he'd gotten furious and lost his mind. He raised his voice, snatched the papers from my hands and didn't talk to me for three nights in a row. Ammi Hamdan is not embarrassed to tell his story in front of us. He is not embarrassed to mention the details. Amer gives us the impression that he doesn't care and that he's at peace with the story about his color and about where he came from. But in the middle of his historic anger—he who's always sought my approval with all the effort he could muster—I became certain that Amer was still nursing a very deep wound.

He picked up his suitcase and left. I stayed by the door watching him walk away, as he periodically turned to glance at me, waving his hand or smiling. His car departed. He made sure to lock the main gate after exiting by clicking the remote control. I felt the devastation of his absence and the absence of Raya and Yusuf all at once. I went up to the second floor. I noticed the mural that I had promised Raya and Yusuf would be ready before they graduated college in Australia. I had been drawing on the wall that extended between their bedrooms since they decided to travel together. I forbade Raya from traveling by herself. She reminded me that I had traveled alone to Egypt in the early nineties. I ignored her pleas. I asked her to wait for Yusuf to graduate so that they could travel together. She was annoyed, but she accepted the situation and didn't defy me. The moment we said goodbye Raya hugged me hard as I cried like I'd never cried in my entire life. She said, "Ma, whenever you miss us, you should paint on the wall outside of our bedrooms."

I painted happy things. Lost stories. Death. Life. I painted my longing for them. My longing for Amer. The mural swelled with stories about me and about them and about the world around us. I don't do realistic paintings. I quit making those very early on. I didn't have the patience for them. I paint my personal chaos, and I think outside the painting. Strokes here and others there. I step away from the painting so I can see it. That's what we should always do. Step away a little, so we can see things clearly, outside of our togetherness with them.

I never keep track of time. The colors spread themselves hungrily on the wall. I don't have a plan regarding my painting. When my yearning for Raya increased, I painted giving birth to her. One detail sticks in my memory from that far-off experience. I had painted my soul hanging from the ceiling. My soul wouldn't return to my chest so I could rest, nor go to heaven so I could calm down. With time, I forgot the pain of labor. I forgot the killer contractions. But I never forgot my hanging soul. I never forgot what it means for one of us to be swinging between life and death, with no choice for either. Life and death, both so close yet remote at the same time. I painted Yusuf's eyes that I loved so much. His mischievous, childish look. Yusuf who licked his bloody fingers the moment he was born before feeding from my breast. I laughed after a fit of tremendous pain.

Amer laughed and said, "The little devil. He drank the blood before his mother's milk."

I painted the shadow of a man's head bending over the shadow of a woman's shoulders. Oh, how delighted I am by these two shadows. They sum up my relationship with Amer. I remember the wedding night. My white dress. I was the first girl to wear a white dress in our village. I had brought it with me from Egypt when Amer and I decided to get married. My dress and veil were met with much disapproval, and there were those who said it was haram, forbidden, and that it was an act of Western imitation. I didn't pay any attention to them. I was happy with the dress and veil that revealed my hair and its accessories. I saw envy in the eyes of spiteful women.

"This girl has gone too far with her strange antics, since the day she started desiring the love of Swahilis," a woman nearby commented.

I was the first girl in my village to sit on a loveseat during her wedding. I designed it myself at the carpenter's exactly as I had imagined it, based on the black and white movies. The carpenter didn't execute it perfectly, but I later decorated it with flowers as

I had dreamed it up. Amer sat beside me, and he even took out a ring from a box and put it on my finger so everybody could see. All hell broke loose. For over five years, our wedding, especially my "lack of manners" and "boldness," were the talk of the town. A few years later, the contagion spread like a wildfire, and we saw dresses of all shapes and colors. A very small number of girls were now wearing the traditional, green Omani dress and staying in a separate room until the grooms' family arrived to accompany them. But I digress. For the first time, I asked myself why there isn't a story that pertained to my mother on this wall. Why isn't there even a tiny detail in reference to my father? To my siblings? To anything from my childhood! My father got into the habit of beating me and my siblings. He would grab a branch from the palm tree, strip the leaves off the branch, and proceed with his harsh task. With or without a reason. My mother would always take his side and say, "If you don't raise them right, then who will?"

My mother was always annoyed with me. She had little patience for me. Maybe because I collected junk. I would save my old dolls and wouldn't throw away any of my stuff. My room and closet were almost overflowing with things. I would move some of the things into storage, where I would check up on them from time to time, dusting them and making sure that everything was in its right place. In my childhood, I used to feel repulsed by drawing and colors. I felt that they were just trash that should be disposed of. My teacher, Ablah Safaa changed my perspective. She noticed my absent-mindedness and short attention span in her class. My constant desire to spend the time during her session in the bathroom. Ablah Safaa spoke with a tender voice. Her fair skin was spotless, and she wore a different colorful skirt every day. Her voice was warm. Her heart was big. She wore a ring on her left hand that she said was a gift from her husband. I told her, "My mother doesn't wear a ring like that." Ablah Safaa laughed. She gave me the courage to start drawing. She made me understand that drawing was a magical game that transformed a blank canvas into stories. I loved stories. I wished for my mother to have Ablah Safaa's voice and her skirt and her voice and her ring. I was the quiet type. I rarely complained. I drew my father huge, and my mother almost as huge as him. Ablah Safaa would ask me, "Where are you, Zahiyya? I don't see you in the picture."

"I'm not here," I would tell her. "I'm in space."

She would laugh and say, "Your drawing is mind blowing." I went to school just so I could see Ablah Safaa's face. I would look for her. Every day, I showed her a new picture, and she would say, "You're an artist," making my heart glow. She also told me, "You know what, girl? If you go to Egypt, Mother of the World, you will learn the true art of drawing." I hid that wish in my heart. I would repeat this wish secretly, in my daily prayers, on "Laylat al-Qadr, the Night of Destiny," on my birthday, and on New Year's Eve. I cried so hard when Ablah Safaa left. The only things that she left me were a box of colors and a sketchbook. She left and returned to Cairo. She said one sentence that kept growing in my heart and mind until this day, "There's nothing like drawing that puts us at ease, Zahiyya."

I loved drawing, but I hated when colors stuck to me. I was always careful. Always organized. I would take many precautionary measures before starting to draw. My classmates would laugh at me as I wiped down the chair and table before sitting. They would comment, "The princess arrived. The princess took a seat. The princess left." I didn't pay any attention to them. My friend Tarfa was all I needed, and then the two of us met Hind. Not once did they ask me a question that bothered me. Our friendship was everlasting. We always stayed in touch, despite going to different schools.

I didn't like the new drawing teacher, Ablah Hayam. She would get upset when I drew long hands and huge fingers—those that my father constantly plastered across my back. She would tell me, "Girl, when are you finally going to learn to control this man's proportions?" But I never learned to do that. I would draw him as a huge man, with prominent teeth and big hands. My mother was kind and tender. She worried about me. She would sometimes indicate to me that she loved me, but there were too many of us in the house. Her constant fear of scandal made her encourage my father to hit us more. At first, I used to think that all fathers were like mine, but when Tarfa told me at school one day that she didn't remember her father ever hitting her, I had to hold back my tears. And when I arrived home, I locked myself in the bathroom and cried until I thought there were no more tears left in my eyes. My father believed in breaking us down. He always saw us as children who never grew up. Every time my father hit me, I would count my fingers and toes for fear that one of them had gone missing.

I climbed the stairs leading up to the roof and then went down. I counted the stairs, one by one. I counted the yellow circles on the living room rug. I stepped on them in a systematic manner, counting them more than once. I put my hand over my mouth, feeling a serious desire to curse my father and mother. I didn't know why those filthy words insisted on exiting my mouth. I repressed them, holding them in my chest. I forbade them from going beyond the borders of my thoughts. In my teenage years, I started to see my father's body naked. I imagined my mother naked. I would shake my head. I was too shy to divulge my thoughts to anyone, even Ablah Safaa to whom I still sent letters and drawings at her mailing address in Egypt. On the street, my head would not stop picturing the bodies of passersby without their clothes on. I would close my eyes and run so I could get over those stupid thoughts.

I don't know why my father didn't crush my skull after he found out that I had signed up behind his back for scholarships. He didn't crush my skull when I went with Tarfa and her brother to Muscat and obtained a scholarship to Egypt. I expected anything from him. Beating. Cursing. Expulsion. I had concocted a few scenarios in my head, and I was completely ready even though my heart was shaking inside my tiny body. But I didn't expect silence from my father, the mighty Musabbih al-Kayumi. I later learned from my mother that the sheikh had talked to him and said, "She'll raise the profile of the tribe. Let her go."

I don't know if that statement was convincing enough for my father. But I was sure that my father wouldn't contest a word uttered by the sheikh. I didn't hear my father's voice. My mother was reprimanded by her friends. They said to her, "The girl will stray and become deviant. Travel corrupts." My mother listened to what people were saying, while my father remained silent as he made my travel arrangements.

I rode on an airplane for the first time in my life. My heart raced. I squeezed into my seat on the plane operated by Gulf Airlines. I recited Ayat al-Kursi, the Throne Verse. I recited several other verses and the prayer for protection and safety while traveling. Every part of my body was shivering. My fingers. My restless legs.

My teeth clattered against one another. A flight attendant noticed my tensed-up body. She asked me if I was cold, and I replied with a "yes." She brought me a blanket and asked me to sit up straight and fasten my seatbelt. I checked that it was fastened over fifty times. I held the blanket tight as I listened to the instructions about safety and emergency exits. I panicked in my seat. "What if we fall?" I shook off my fears by praying and reading the Quran and clinging tightly to the blanket. I felt my soul's delight when we soared, and I watched Oman get smaller and smaller until it vanished.

I tasted the flavor of freedom. Doing things without anyone seeing me. But I didn't really do anything worth mentioning. My mothers' obsessions with scandal followed me like a curse. I got a room in an apartment with three Omani women and a Bahraini student. The only problem I faced had to do with the common kitchen and bathroom. I put up a shelf in my room, and I stocked it with some tea and sugar, a kettle, and some cooking utensils. A small gas stove for preparing tea and light meals. I wouldn't enter their kitchen. But I had to share with them the apartment's one bathroom. The other thing I never told anyone about were my visits to Dr. Ibrahim Abd al-Jaleel's clinic in the al-Muhandiseen neighborhood. Those weren't exactly treatment sessions. We would talk to each other like friends. Fine. He tricked me with this whole friendship business and lured me into talking with him. During the rare occasions that Dr. Ibrahim—whom I referred to as Ammu Ibrahim out of respect— saw me with his daughter Ula in the hall of the Fine Arts College in Zamalek, he saw something and said, "You are talented beyond the norm." I believed him at first. Then I understood that he meant something else by "beyond the norm." There was something abnormal in you is what he meant. I liked Ammu Ibrahim more than I liked his daughter Ula. Ammu Ibrahim's house was the only Egyptian house that I ever set foot and had meals in. Ammu Ibrahim would put his arms around the shoulders of Ula's mother, Khaltu Umm Ula. And Khaltu Umm Ula would gently press on his fingers from time to time. Moustapha made jokes over lunch. Ula laughed. The family laughed. I tried hard to laugh with them. Ammu Ibrahim would get up from his seat around the table and insist on loading up my plate with food. He insisted that I eat the delicious kushari that Khaltu Umm Ula prepared. I preferred the mulukhiyya greens. It was the most delicious thing that entered my stomach in Egypt.

Ammu Ibrahim didn't prescribe any medication for me. Just deep breathing and relaxing in his chair, and the stories that grew between us. I asked Ammu Ibrahim, "Am I sick?" He laughed in a loud voice. His beautiful dimple moved, as he said, "You're the most beautiful storyteller in the world." I felt that diaspora was exactly like drawing. It eased the rhythm of my life that teemed with rules. I was helping myself do things that I wasn't used to doing before. My anxiety became less severe. I stopped counting things and imagining naked people. What I did was start to draw my thoughts and fears as Ammu Ibrahim told me to: "Draw whatever you're thinking about." I drew my mother naked and my father naked and other people naked, and I stopped thinking about their bodies. I drew the stairs and the circles on the rug, so I stopped counting them. A stain here and there. I laughed to myself and said, "The princess has left her palace."

When Amer is away on travel, I don't like leaving the house very much, unless the situation requires buying necessities for the house. Faneesh and I went out together. I wrote a list of things we needed. Then the shopping mission began. I kept an eye on the vegetables and fruit that Faneesh picked. Sometimes I would grab the bag from her hands and pick the vegetables myself in front of her. She learned quickly, and my heart was delighted. Faneesh didn't know what these little things did to me. I invited my girlfriends to dinner at my house. I killed the time that went so slowly with them. I started the cooking mission. I love cooking. For me, it's like decorating scarves, arranging seashells. I cook with passion. I grilled fish. I prepared biryani, kabouli, makbous, salona, haris, and arsiyya with a skill unmatched by anyone. Faneesh's curiosity led her to spy on my magical ways in the kitchen. My special mixes. I didn't give her the opportunity. I kept her busy and away from me. I love decorating things. Every dish that leaves my hand is like a painting. My girlfriends were delighted by the atmosphere at the nightly gathering, by dishes they wouldn't dream of tasting in the most refined hotels in the world. This is the only positive thing that I remember getting from my mother. She pushed me into the kitchen early on. She taught me everything so she could rest, and so I surpassed her. Cooking and drawing and travel are three things that changed my life. I designed a complete training course for Raya and Yusuf in the kitchen before they left for Australia. They complained in the beginning. But they ultimately recognized the value of what I had done when they found themselves in the throes of the experience.

I reached my bed, spent. I looked at the picture sitting on the end table. In the picture from our last trip to Thailand, Amer is wrapping his arms around my shoulders on one side and around Yusuf's and Raya's shoulders on the other. The four of us are smiling, waterfall and greenery behind us. I closed my eyes. Sleep seemed to flee from them. My bed was cold, with no life in it. No pillow talk. No arms to take me into a soft stupor. No body to shield me from the brutality of the pale, switched-off world. There was no flavor to my days, nor smell.

It was during those moments that I remembered the papers that I had left on the end table. The story of Bi Soura, as my father-in-law had told it and as Amer had written it. I prepared a big cup of milk tea with ginger. I sat on the swing on the balcony where Amer often read. I turned on the light and started reading the papers.

I paid a high price for being the eldest son. I cried a lot. My father spanked me and said, "Men don't cry like women." I emigrated from Oman to Africa with my father in search of a better life. That was in the early fifties, and I was twelve years old. I kept myself from turning around to see the face of my mother who was falling apart, or the faces of my siblings that swelled with tears.

We lived in the village of Fuoni, which is located in Unguja. Life there was as glorious as could be. My father first worked in a grocery store. My father was very short-tempered. He would get frustrated with Africans, Indians, Banyans and all kinds of people whose ethnicities had nothing to do with Arabs. He treated them as a superior would. He would get angry at me for merely addressing them in their language, Swahili, since I had picked up a few words. His blood would boil. He would yell in my face, "The children of black Zanjal are making you forget your own language."

People in town started boycotting my father's store because of how badly he treated them. He incurred a huge loss, so we didn't have enough money to send to our family. During one of the gatherings for Omanis, a rich man of Omani heritage made my father an offer to come work on his plantation, to oversee his private "shamba." My father welcomed the offer. We left Fuoni and headed to Manga Pwani. I didn't know what a shamba was until I saw it with my own eyes. A vast piece of land. It had trees of all shapes and kinds, like coconut, mango, and banana, and spices like black pepper and cinnamon. Clove trees covered a large space of the shamba as well. The name of the area was well-suited for my father. Manga Pwani. Pwani meaning "sea." Manga refers to fundamentalist Omanis. It's a coastal area that has farms, fishing spots, and Omani enclaves— more than the ones found in Fuoni.

Our house was located inside the shamba, and for the first time in my life, I saw houses that were made of brick and had roofs. During my entire life in Oman, specifically in Samael, I had only seen houses made of mud, stone, or palm leaves. Now I had a bed and a seat. Both were made from local wood.

Vendors would pass by Manga Pwani on their mopeds, and each one had a special voice that set him apart from the others. One would sell meat, a second sold chicken, a third sold roti bread, and a fourth sold fruit. I almost memorized the voice of each one of them, distinguishing it from the others. I would go outside whenever we needed to buy something.

Twice a year my father would take me to Malindi, which was part of Zanzibar. There, I visited the souqs and was stunned by how civilized the city was. I heard later that Sultan Jamshid was forced to surrender the city to Kenya shortly before the coup.

My father finally lost some of his defensiveness in Manga Pwani. His fears eased. I found people to talk to in Omani dialect. I would run around with open arms in the field where we worked. I ran until

HUDA HAMED

the smell of cloves filled my heart and soul. We started to make a good
profit. We had a small fortune, enough to send for the rest of the family.
I was delighted about that and remained hopeful that I would see my
mother and siblings.

Sleep overpowered me. I felt tremendous exhaustion invading my body. I tucked the papers in the white folder. I put the folder on the end table next to me. My phone finally rang.

"Hello, Amer. How are you? I've been worried about you, umri, my life. Put my mind at ease."

"Don't be worried. I made it to Tanzania. I'm on my way to the hotel. I miss you."

"I miss you more. Amer, I started reading your novel."

"This makes me happy, Zahiyya."

"You know me. I'm slow at reading, but I'm enjoying it."

"That's the most important thing."

"Take care of yourself."

I hung up the phone. I closed my eyes and fell into a deep sleep.

I woke up earlier than usual with a headache. Two Panadols and milk tea did the trick. I couldn't go back to sleep. I put on a scarf over my nightgown. I stood in front of the mural. I had stocked a side shelf with an electric kettle and all the supplies needed to make tea and coffee any time. I quickly prepared a cup of milk tea that I flavored with rose water in my bedroom. I took a few sips and contemplated what I had painted the day before. The tea made me feel better. I thought about the necessity of keeping the white space surrounding the shadow of the head leaning over the shoulder. I considered adding a small detail close to Yusuf's mischievous eyes.

But would that thing—that looked like rising steam—resemble my soul that once hung in the ceiling of the delivery room? I wasn't quite sure yet.

I went downstairs. I concealed my happiness. Everything was exactly as I liked. I did not want Faneesh to know that I was pleased with her. That day marked the end of her first month. I handed her the salary in an envelope. Her face lit up as if she was in disbelief, yet it was the smallest salary I had ever paid a maid. The salaries of my Indonesian maids ranged between seventy and eighty riyals, and those of Filipinas ranged between eighty and one hundred twenty. Darsheen's salary reached one hundred and fifty riyals in her ninth year. Based on the contract, I paid Faneesh sixty riyals. That bothered Amer.

"The work is the same," he said. "Why is her salary less?"

"It's definitely not because she's Ethiopian, or Black!"

"Then, why, Zahiyya? If this is about education, she's educated and has experience. You know she's worked at three other houses before coming here."

"That's her salary, based on the contract! And, she's agreed to it."

Faneesh did not wish to go out on her day off. I told her that payday was on the twenty-third of every month and that it would be her vacation day. I told her to go wherever she wanted. Faneesh got nervous and said calmly, "Madame, I don't know where I'd go. Do you mind if I just stay here?"

What else would I want more than for you to stay, Faneesh? Of course, I didn't mind. But what would Amer say if he found out that I had revoked the only humane space that I allowed maids, as he would say? What would Raya and Yusuf say, they who have always voraciously defended the rights of this oppressed group of people, as they called them? What would Hind and Tarfa say? The two of them were always telling me, "Despite all your severity, you get credit for the monthly vacation you give maids."

I asked her, "Faneesh, why don't you want to go out?"

"I don't know this place very well. I wasn't used to going out in Saudi except with the lady of the house. Same for Dubai."

My heart was delighted. It was her personal choice. I didn't force her to do anything. She wanted that. What could I do? Of course, I wasn't going to force her to do something she didn't want to do. Breathing a sigh of relief, I said to her, "OK, Faneesh. That's up to you. If you like, take the day off. No need for you to do any work."

She smiled. "No, Madame . . . I'd like to spend my day as usual."

I scored a goal in everybody's net—Amer's, Yusuf's, Raya's, Hind's, and Tarfa's. I had not forbidden her from going out. I had not asked her to work on her day off. She was the one who wanted to, and she did it with a smile. Faneesh kept quiet, staying out of the guests' way, and took care of everything. The house and the yard. She tended the plants with devotion, exactly like Amer did. Her dark-skinned face lit up with a smile the entire time. Her teeth were extremely white. Her appetite for talking was extinguished, and that was what brought happiness to my heart the most. That was despite the fact that Amer had tried to ignite the flames of her stories a few times, but every time, I blew them out with cold air. The stories of maids are tedious and boring. Nothing but their pains and poverty and needs that brought them to us. They open our shopping bags and are astounded by what we have bought. By the amount of money we spend. Whether they like it or not, they are envious, and their hearts are black, and I don't believe anything else. One grocery shopping trip to the City Center costs me three times a maid's monthly salary. A few things cost as much as a maid's salary. My Kipling bag costs more than a maid's salary. My pair of leather shoes costs twice as much as her salary, if not more. I don't allow them to look at or touch my things. They just carry the bags from the car to the bedroom. They are fortunate enough to guess what we've bought. No more, no less. As for grocery items—that go into the kitchen—I remove the prices beforehand to spare them the burden of sorrow. My Indonesian maid Osira once said, "Our children go hungry, while your food goes into the trash." That was her last day in my house. She had come here to envy me, to make her eyes even more squinty than they already were. Amazed, Amer would always ask me, "How do you manage to combine all these contradictions? You fought for your right to get an education, to choose your own husband and to limit yourself to two kids only. You fought against circumcision and against women who just accepted their bad fortunes in life. On the other hand, you are hostile to simple women who have travelled a long way for a small fee, a fee that you make from selling one abaya. And on top of it all, you believe in envy. Are you afraid they would steal the blessings that you possess and that they do not?"

Maids are maids. Whether we like it or not, we can never eradicate their desire that our blessings perish, or that our blessings be transferred to them. Even if they bow to us and smile and show us the utmost respect. Amer does not believe me. He delights their little hearts with his polite words, with some money in their pockets. He listens to them as they wipe down his car before he takes off for work. They tell him about their disgusting lives, and Amer—my little baby who hasn't grown up yet—believes and worries about them. He would listen to the voice of Kazoomi, the Filipina maid, as she cried in the bathroom every morning. He would ask me about her crying. I would tell him, "Ignore her. Ignoring her will yield results." But Amer could not ignore her at all. One day, I woke up to his voice, as he talked to her before going to work. She stood there, embarrassed, as he insisted on knowing the reason behind her daily crying. She told him later that her breasts were hurting because of the milk. She told him that she had left her three-month-old baby to come here for work. The milk trapped in her breasts was giving her a fever, and it hurt every time she tried to squeeze it out over the sink. Amer's face changed. He left quickly and got into his car. Kazoomi had to deal with my wrath and yelling that day. She kept crying and saying, "Mr. Amer wanted to know." That night, Amer returned home with a ticket to the Philippines. I told her, "Adab, that'll teach you some manners. You deserve worse than this." She cried so bitterly that I worried she was going to faint in front of us. Amer said, "This envelope contains your airline ticket and your salary for five months. Go spend time with your child. And then you can decide if you want to come back. My phone number is in the envelope too." Kazoomi's crying bout continued as she grabbed Amer's hand and started kissing it, while he gently withdrew it.

I was upset. I didn't talk to him for a whole day. I had told him over and over again that it was not possible for a relationship of equals to grow between master and servant, but he wouldn't learn anything from me. His little heart couldn't take it, despite being exposed to their thieving, slyness, and lies. One of them seduced him, and a second one—on whom he bestowed gifts generously—fled with her boyfriend, leaving us with no trace of her whereabouts to this day. A third one grew a big belly among us, and we didn't figure out that she was pregnant until she was in her seventh month, when her movement slowed down and her enthusiasm for work and cleaning waned. There were also a fourth and a fifth, and stories with no beginning and no end.

He gave Faneesh some of Raya and Yusuf's English-language books. I saw him treat her with kindness. He asked her to read so that she wouldn't forget what she had learned. It infuriated me, but before erupting in his face, I remembered the necessity of not butting heads with a maid. So I kept it all inside my chest. I saw her during her free time flipping through the books with great attention. I ignored her. I prepared a quick meal for myself. I asked Faneesh to bring it to my bedroom. I lay on the bed and eagerly returned to Amer's novel.

I laughed my ass off, thanks to my father's only remaining tooth. That day, he met me with only one tooth, still hanging in his mouth after the coconut incident. I laughed, but this time my father couldn't hit me, which made me pity him. It was a painful accident that landed him in a hospital bed for three months. My loud-voiced, hot-tempered father—who treated the black Africans arrogantly—was yelling at the workers, instructing them about the importance of not slacking off or talking to one another while harvesting coconuts. While my father was doling out advice and obscenities to one of the workers who was at the top of a coconut tree, the angry worker tossed down a big branch that was loaded with over twenty coconuts. The branch landed directly on my father's head; his face was busted, and all his teeth fell out, except for that one tooth that stood as a witness to the accident.

HUDA HAMED

I loved the food that the generous neighbors would send us. I loved muhogo, which our neighbor prepared with meat. I loved ugali and the mikate ya kusukuma. I loved their women, draped in bright colors. There were only two things that terrified me throughout my stay in Zanzibar. First, there were the stories told about "Alwa Makonda," the cannibals. It was said that as soon as one of them fell ill, he would be turned into a delicious meal. I would shiver all night upon hearing about one of their adventures. But lucky for me, they lived on the far edges of the country. The other thing that made me pee my pants several times was the Chatu snake. It was as big as the trunk of a coconut tree. I saw that snake three times during the sixteen years I spent in Zanzibar. The first time, my father and I were at the shamba during the coconut harvest season, and my father was supervising the workers. I sat down to rest on a trunk that was surrounded by grass. I felt the softness of the trunk as soon as I relaxed my buttocks on it. I felt its breath and the warm blood in its veins, and I became more certain that it was a snake when it started moving. One of the workers started screaming, "Chatu, Chatu," when he saw it raise its head. I ran with all my might in the opposite direction of the workers who charged in its direction in order to kill it. The second time, I entered the kitchen to find half a Chatu dangling from the ventilation window, its giant mouth gaping. My loud cry brought my father with the shotgun. As soon as he fired a bullet between its eyes, its strength diminished. A large number of shamba workers pulled it away from the window of our house. They chopped it into small pieces that maybe ended up in their stomachs. The third time was a killer. We were picking cloves. It was the custom to wrap ourselves with a piece of cloth, tying two sides of the cloth around the waist and the other two sides around the neck, creating some sort of a bag with two open spaces on the right and the left. Through those open sides, we stuffed the fresh cloves that we picked and then took for drying, in the next stage of the process, before exporting them. We would first tie the clove tree with a piece of fabric, and laborers, women, and children would then sit on top of it so the harvesting process could begin. I had asked one of the laborers to help me up a tree so I could help them pick cloves. I landed on a soft body, I didn't see any cloves. Just rings inside rings inside rings of a huge Chatu body. The Chatu raised its head next to mine. Its breath was so close that it hit me in the face. I fell from atop the tree like a shooting star.

My skin crawled. I hate snakes. I felt them crawl all over my body. Watching me from somewhere. I looked up to see that they had escaped the pages. I screamed when my phone rang.

"Amer, dear, how are you?"

"Zahiyya, I miss you."

"Are you in Dodoma now?"

"I left the hotel in the morning. I'm currently in Nguga, the biggest island in Zanzibar. My father Hamdan was here in the fifties. I'll be leaving to Manga Pwani later."

"Great, Amer. But how are you going to begin your search?"

"I don't know, Zahiyya. I made a deal with a translator, and people here are nice. They take a look at my face and are initially surprised, but once they hear my broken Swahili their surprise dissipates."

"Amer, I hope you find Bi Soura for Ammi Hamdan's sake and yours."

"Ameen."

"Are you enjoying the place?"

"It rains all the time."

"Don't get wet. You'll catch a cold."

"This place is gorgeous, Zahiyya. The color green surrounds everything. The smell of cloves fills me up, just like it used to fill my father's lungs. I saw houses in Middle Eastern, Indian, and African styles."

"Amazing, my love!"

"Zahiyya, next time you'll come with me, and we'll go to the House of Wonders together."

"I heard about the House of Wonders on the radio."

"There's one thing that I couldn't resist and that I tried without you."

"What's that?"

"The Fordhani Gardens."

"What is *that?*"

"Local popular dishes. They're the best."

"You know it would be impossible for me to go near them. Halal 'alek, they're all yours."

"I also drank sugar cane. I've never tasted anything like it in my life."

"Have fun, Amer! You're living it up like nobody's business."

"Habibti, my darling. I bought you tinga tinga and kangas and tanzanite."

"You're such a fast learner. What are those? Food?"

"No, not food. Things you'd like. Tinga tinga are drawings, and kangas are traditional headscarves, and as for tanzainte, they're colored stones. I'm sure you'll find the right places for them in our home."

"Ya salaam, my, oh, my! I'm excited to see them, and to see you."

"Very soon, precious."

"Take care of yourself."

I was delighted to hear Amer's voice. Something in my heart took off in a direction I didn't know and came back to me, panting. I rolled onto my back and felt happy. I resumed reading Ammi Hamdan's diaries with even more passion.

My father wouldn't give up on wearing the traditional Omani dishdasha. He'd show it off, and I would wear one just like his. Every time my father would find out that one of his friends was planning on going to Oman, he would give him some shillings and request that he bring us back some Omani dishdashas from there. The Omani women here would sew dishdashas and trousers at home for their girls, and they would put the leso on their heads. I would see them in their clothes, and my mother's and sisters' faces would jump out at me. I would wipe my tears with the sleeve of my dishdasha, before my father's slap would fall on my back and remind me, as usual, that I was a man and that tears were not created for men. On official occasions, my father would wear a koti on top of his Omani dishdasha, to mark the importance of the event. He carried a cane in his hand. He would take out his most beloved dagger and meticulously place it on his waist. My father walked as if he were the king, or as if the whole world were walking along with him, and he wouldn't stop repeating the story of our prominent origin and the purity of our lineage in front of everyone he met at these social occasions that were attended by Omanis from different places.

My heart hurt as I watched the boys going to school. They walked, laughed, flipped through their books, and learned English, Swahili,

and Quran recitation while I sat in the shamba among the workers. I
told my father several times of my wish to get an education, but he would
turn his face away from me as if he didn't even see me. I would open
the window in the morning to hear them recite the national anthem.
I'd stare at their books. I tried to get my father's heart to soften, but he
would get frustrated with me. I saw the children deciphering words.
They spoke English with amazing speed. Mohammad al-Hanai, the
son of my father's friend, who was five years younger than me, entered
school. He learned to write his name in Arabic and English. During
one of our visits to their home, Mohammad showed me his books and
notebooks. I almost cried. Mohammad's father showed off his child's
educational accomplishments in front of my father. I told myself that
maybe that conversation might change my father's preconceptions about
mixed schools. My father got edgy and said angrily:

"I came here to make a living. I didn't bring my son so he could run
around with the children of Zanjal."

We left and never set foot again in Mohammad al-Hanai's home.
My father rarely talked to him during official occasions. He would
repeat, "Abu Mohammad ruined his son."

After a long argument, my father told me, "If you want to go to
Sheikh Marhoun al-Khalili's to learn the Quran, it's not a problem.
But studying with the children of Zanjal is a no-no."

Many Omanis engaged with the general population of Zanzibar;
they didn't set forth the type of tough terms that my vicious father
did regarding any possibility of my being in contact with them. For
my father, the school was the biggest environment for chaos. I went to
Sheikh Marhoun al-Khalili, an Omani man who couldn't find a job
better than teaching the Omani boys and converts how to pray and

read the Quran. I told him I wanted to learn how to read and write, in addition to the Quran. So he said to me, "How much will you pay?" Color drained from my face.

Smiling, he said, "I will teach you how to read and write in return for you sweeping my house and washing my clothes and doing anything else that I ask of you after the session."

I nodded in agreement and began my journey. I would work with my father at the shamba, and in the afternoon, I would study with Sheikh Marhoun and then serve him afterward. The type of services I provided changed every day with the changing needs of the widowed sheikh, and I was patient with his requests. The worst request that he asked of me was washing his clothes. I didn't like their smell. He would put a lot of lotions and ointments on his body, which would cling to his clothes. I would bring the harita plant and soak it in water. It foamed and smelled exactly like soap. I would then start washing his clothes. But thanks to the constant rains, Sheikh Marhoun's clothes wouldn't dry easily. So I would line-dry them inside his house and light up some coals underneath them so that they would dry faster. I learned that from the African workers at the shamba. Those times reminded me of Oman's sun. I would leave the valley drenched in water, and it would take just a few seconds for my clothes to dry.

Pangs of hunger suddenly struck me. I thought about making a mouth-watering chicken kabsa. I treaded lightly into the kitchen. Faneesh had put the chicken in a bowl of water to let it thaw. She had diced for me some potatoes, onions, tomatoes, and peppers in equal sizes. I soaked the rice in water. I turned on some music and let it seep into the kitchen. Faneesh stood near me. She was almost sticking to me. I felt her breath near me, as if she was

HUDA HAMED

about to open her mouth to say something. I ignored her as she waited for me to raise my head. I kept myself busy preparing the food. Her standing there made me nervous. I eventually raised my head in her direction, so I could push my nervousness away from me.

"What is it, Faneesh?"

"Madame . . . I."

"Didn't we already agree that talking is not allowed?"

"I have a question."

"Questions aren't allowed either."

She stopped talking. But she didn't leave the kitchen. She remained in place, smothering me with her silence.

"What, Faneesh? What questions do you have?"

"Madame, did anyone else live in this house before you?"

"What? How is this any of your business?"

She lowered her voice. She looked like she was about to tell me a dangerous secret.

"I think there's a woman who committed suicide in this house."

"What? What's this nonsense? If you don't want to lose your livelihood, you better swallow your tongue."

Faneesh resumed washing the dishes beside me. Her question gnawed at me. My curiosity grew.

"What makes you think there's a woman who committed suicide in my house?" I asked her.

"The dream, Madame. It's a dream I've been having, but you don't want to hear about it. I can't bear this secret on my own anymore."

She turned and looked me straight in the eye. My heart raced, while I maintained a stern look on my face. She stood facing me directly, wiping her hands with the apron that sat on top of her blue uniform.

"Madame, I dream of her footsteps as she climbs from the bottom of the stairs to the second floor. Her breath rises and mixes with her crying, and her pulse quickens as if it's right next to my ears. Her feet are bare. Her long dress flows over her running legs, revealing them at times and concealing them at others. She reaches the second floor. Her arms collide with the air. Then, she charges towards the rail of the balcony with all the speed she can muster. I jump from my bed. I catch my breath. My whole body drips with sweat. I look out my bedroom window. There is no corpse under the balcony. I call upon the Virgin Mary. Then I ward off the devil as Hajjah Moudi had taught me in Saudi. I try so hard to control my exhaustion, my panting. It's as if I had been running with the suicidal woman. As if I had been with her."

The tone of Faneesh's voice changed. She looked scared. I, too, believed in dreams and was terrified of them. But it was a trap. I was sure it was a trap that she had set for me so that I would open the window to talking between us. I wasn't going to fall for her stupid trick.

"Madame, I find it hard to sleep. The women's feet and her panting haunt me. I had this dream four times in the exact same detail."

"Faneesh, these are meaningless dreams. There's no truth to them."

"I don't want to cause any trouble, Madame. My family needs every riyal I send home. But . . . "

"I don't want to hear these stories ever again."

Silence sat between us. The kitchen quieted down. I went on preparing my favorite *kabsa*, while my brain drew the details of Faneesh's dream. I ate while flipping through the TV channels in the big living room. My mind was preoccupied between Ammi Hamdan's story and Amer's trip and Faneesh's dream. I finished my food. I thought about drawing on the sheilahs. Maybe that would take the burden of thinking off me.

I spread out the sheilah on the table and let the colors expand over it. I don't like the color black. This is my little war against darkness. I give drab women some color. My mother, my mother's mother, and my grandmother's mother before them used to dress in bright colors in Oman. They would make sure the colors on their sheilahs matched those at the "sinjaf," the bottom part of the sleeves of their dishdashas. The dishdasha was usually knee-length, and they wore trousers—that they sewed with their own skillful hands—beneath the dishdasha. They conjured up colors that were inspired by everything in nature from saffron to indigo dye. They loved life. Being able to add color to one's clothing signified good social and economic status. At the end of the nineties, however, black abayas invaded and became a part of us. A manufactured part of our daily life. The woman who didn't wear an abaya now seemed like an apostate. Sick eyes would harass her. Raya didn't wear an abaya initially. My mother was upset at her and would tell her, "People are saying Raya isn't a child anymore." I defended her and tried to protect her choice but at some point, she was infected and started to fluctuate between bright colors and blackness as she pleased, and as fashion recommended.

A red flower, and next to it, a white one and then a violet one grew heavy on the green branch. This time, I was drawing across the sheilah, not at its edges. The client had said she wanted the sheilah to wear at weddings. She requested real gems that wouldn't be ruined by washing. I left the colors to dry. I stood up for a bit to rest my hand and stretch my spine. I looked at my drawing from a distance. It looked stunning. The warm colors longed to hug the gems. I went up to my room. I prepared another cup of tea. This time, I flavored it with thyme. I threw myself on the bed that Faneesh had remade a little while ago. I grabbed Ammi Hamdan's diaries.

During the lesson at Sheikh Marhoun's, I met Bi Soura. An African girl, her parents had converted to Islam recently. She wanted to learn the Quran. She didn't serve Ammi Marhoun like I did. Her family could afford to pay him a few shillings. Bi Soura wore colorful and vibrant outfits, and she said they were made from kitenge fabric. I'd get very shy whenever she started chatting with me, asking about me, my name, and my home country. Her questions and curiosity grew, while I sweated. I felt like someone committing a sin. I don't know if I was acting out of fear of my father who objected to my talking with "the children of Zanjal," or because I wasn't yet able to speak Swahili, although I did understand it very well. Or maybe it was because she was the first girl to enter my world during a critical time of my life. I shielded my eyes from her. I avoided talking to her so she wouldn't discover my fragility. My father had always advised me not to get close to Black girls. He reminded me that my cousin Jokha had been reserved for me since we were five years of age, and that her father never married her off for that reason. Bi Soura's family also warned her against getting close to us Arabs for fear that she would be dragged and sold as a slave in the Gulf, just like cloves and coconuts and dried fruit were sold; but if marriage was the intention, then that was something they highly welcomed, or rather it was a source of pride.

I couldn't resist Bi Soura's beauty. It seemed that she was also attracted to me. Her tenderness charmed me, her body that had ripened prematurely. Her violet color, her vivacious spirit that gave my life taste and color. Her beautiful voice as she sang: "Koti wkoti, wmanazi wmanazi, wjinji wbimi wmtaitama." She showed a keen interest in fashion, just like Western women, something that I wasn't used to seeing in Oman. In Zanzibar, people drew bold designs, and many of them were adorned with Swahili expressions and resembled in their bright colors what the residents of Hawaii wore.

In Sheikh Marhoun al-Khalili's house we would meet, and passion grew between us every day. We got into many conversations. I told her about Oman. About our mud house, about my young siblings. About the palm trees. And when Sheikh Marhoun noticed the fever in our bodies, he watched us more closely, and I worried that he might snitch on me to my father, who strove to hold on to our Omani identity. He strove to force me into a vortex of isolation that I couldn't stand anymore.

Sheikh Marhoun sat me down and told me that I would be headed toward my doom if I surrendered to my lust. I told him that my father had deprived me of an education just so I wouldn't mix with the children of Africans, so how was I supposed to be honest with him about my desire to marry an African woman. He said to me, "Marrying you two in the presence of two witnesses and keeping your secret is easier on me than you falling into sin, Hamdan." That hellish idea of his had

not occurred to me. I urged him to hasten with implementing it. Bi
Soura accepted, and her family agreed to keep our secret safe among us.
They didn't ask much of me.

Bi Soura became my beloved, the halal way. Dread withdrew from
our hearts, and we no longer feared blame.

We began the adventure of meeting secretly at the house of her
family, who received me with some suspicion and also some friendliness.
I would meet Bi Soura, and she would pull me by my hand—which
was planted in hers—and tell me as she looked at the sea outside her
bedroom window, "Hamdan, the sea foam looks just like sugar." I liked
my name better when it rolled off her tongue. My father insisted that
I wear the dishdasha, with the wazar wrapped around it, and that I
speak in Arabic, but Swahili words and songs started to trickle from my
heart and from my lips every time I met Bi Soura, and my heart grew
more attached to her.

During the times stolen from my work hours at the house of Sheikh
Marhoun al-Khalili's house after our lessons, and in her small, tidy
room, we met as lovers. We would touch, and like wood, our bodies fed
the fires of our passion. My supple whiteness covered her silky reddish-
black skin, and her killer curves. I would slip my hands under her
braided hair, and she would take my lips, which had never tasted
lips before hers, in little bites. When time besieged us, we became more
gluttonous as our heartbeats and senses awakened. We never had
enough of our game.

My strong friendship with Saeed al-Mahrouqi, who worked with his
father in the export business, saved me. Politics, books, and the clove
trade brought us together. I used going out with him as a pretext, and he
would always conspire with me and bless my secret trysts. That was how
I fabricated lies and tricks so I could have a blessed piece of paradise.

Ya Ilahi, oh my God. How had Ammi Hamdan done such a deed, despite the fact that his father was such a hotheaded fanatic? How had he let his desires and yearnings grow in hiding? An overwhelming longing woke up in my body for Amer. I wished he would return home quickly. I folded the papers and put them back in the white envelope. I thought about taking a short nap but resisted. A nap would destroy my night's sleep. I called Raya and Yusuf to check on them. They talked to me quickly as if they were running, as if they were having a "fast food" meal. The house was depressing without them all.

ELEVEN

I WENT DOWN the stairs. Faneesh was out of sight. The best thing I had done when designing the layout for the house was to put the maid's bedroom and bathroom next to the kitchen so that our shared space would be minimal. Faneesh came out in her blue uniform and a mop in her hand. She was mopping the living room floor. I didn't hear the sound of her footsteps because it was absorbed by the soft cotton slippers she was wearing. I noticed that her face was pale, and her movements seemed slower than usual. I didn't pay her any attention. I turned on the TV. She continued cleaning without lifting her head. Without smiling. That was a depressing sign, for it's a very bad omen when the maid doesn't smile. I flipped through the channels. Her black face disappeared. Then it came closer again. She was looking for another opportunity to speak. She definitely wasn't going to get it. She left the living room to go to the hallway. I caught my breath. I called Hind. Hind asked me to go with her to the souq. I could hear the commotion around her, so it seemed like a bad time to continue the conversation. I hung up. I called Tarfa. She was relaxed, as usual. She was drinking coffee and eating a big bunch of dates. She could sense my anxiety.

"What's going on, Zahiyya?" She asked. "Is there a new stain, or did Faneesh turn out to be worse than you expected?"

"It's neither of those things," I said. "I'm going to tell you something, but please don't laugh."

"I won't laugh."

"Faneesh has been dreaming of a suicidal woman in my house."

Tarfa burst out laughing. I stopped talking until she resumed listening to me.

"This is serious, Tarfa," I said. "The dream keeps recurring, she says. And it looks like it's starting to affect her."

"Zahiyya," she said. "Try to be sensible. It's just a dream, but . . . "

"But what?"

"What's strange is that you're so concerned."

"No, I'm not concerned. I just wanted to talk to someone about it."

"OK, let's go out."

"No, I'm busy," I said. "With the mural, the sheilahs. It's hard."

"Aha. OK, as you wish."

I wasn't busy with anything. Boredom was killing me. Faneesh's face, like her dream, was starting to gnaw at my nerves. Faneesh came in again. She looked me in the eye. She put the mop in the bucket. She approached me.

"Madame, are you sure that no one has committed suicide in this house?"

"Faneesh, I can't take your questions anymore."

"I have a splitting headache," she said. "Madame, I'm tired."

"This is the last time we talk about this."

"But the scenario is repeating itself."

"Get out of here," I said. "I don't want to see your face today."

She picked up the bucket. The top part of the mop danced as she did that. She closed her eyes as she was about to tear up. She closed the living room door. I called Amer. My hands were trembling. My heart leaped from its place.

"Hala habibti, hello my love."

"Amer. Amer. I."

"What's going on?"

"I'm scared. Faneesh . . . "

"What's the matter with her?" he asked. "Did she run away? Refuse to work? What is it?"

"Faneesh is having dreams."

"What?"

"She's dreaming of a woman committing suicide in our house," I said. "The dream has been recurring."

"Take it easy, habibti Zahiyya," he said. "It's just a dream that reflects her fears."

"That's what I told her," I said. "But she's pale, and she's not eating. I'm worried she's going to run away. Do you think she's using the dream as an excuse?"

"Zahiyya, calm down," he said. "Try to give her a chance. Talk to her. Try to ease her fears of being alone, her silence."

"OK, Amer. I'll talk to you later."

I opened the window. I saw Faneesh watering Amer's trees with a sad face. What could I possibly do about her stupid dream? I put my hands over my heart. I felt my heartbeats, which were now beginning to get back to their normal rhythm. That was enough. I was going to forget about the dream as if it never happened. She too would surely forget about it with time. Her problem wasn't going to be solved. Her problem was nothing like Darsheen's simple problems, which never went beyond school fees, her husband's drinking expenses, the expenses of fixing the toilet at home. It wasn't like Kazoumi's problems— Kazoumi, who worried about hurricanes and floods. Every time those things happened

HUDA HAMED

in the Philippines, we'd put together a fund for her that would spare us her tears and mental breakdowns. How could I solve the problem of the dream except with more silence and arrogance? I fought off my anxiety attack by going up to my room again, by reopening Amer's novel.

I was caught by surprise when my father sent a letter to our family telling them that they shouldn't go through the trouble of traveling from Oman to Zanzibar because we were coming back. Things were starting to change. Sudden death swept the clove trees. One day, a tree would seem perfectly healthy, and then the next day, just like that, its leaves would suddenly dry up, and the tree would die. Disease struck over half of the shamba fields. My father was starting to get sick and tired of the greed of Indian merchants.

One night, my father opened up to me. "We should return to Oman with our little fortune before it evaporates."

Tears nearly fell from my eyes. He looked at me. I told him I didn't want to leave. He kept staring at me inquisitively.

I said courageously, "Father, I am married to Bi Soura, the African woman who has been studying the Quran with me. She's pregnant. Sheikh Marhoun married us before I ever touched her."

All I could feel was the heat of his hands as he slapped me on the face. He kicked me, striking the upper part of my body at times and the lower part at others.

"Son of a bitch," he said. "You've mixed the races, you son of a bitch."

I didn't even bat an eye as he hit me. He kept on hitting me until he'd exhausted all his energy. Tired, he fell to the floor without any resistance on my part.

News about the tense political situation and the rumors that spread here and there pushed my father to call a truce with me.

Some said to us, "Your sultan is Omani, and your rights are going to be preserved. Your prestige is protected. What are you worried about?" Others said, "You should come to an agreement with the African parties to confront the English colonialists." But my father decided that it was important to heed the prophecy of Sheikh Nasser Bin Saeed al-Ismaeli, who sensed a dark future starting to creep over Zanzibar's prosperity. The sheikh sensed a conspiracy and said that he wasn't going to stay in Zanzibar until the day that the African would come and shave off his beard with shards of broken glass. With his sharp eyes, al-Ismaeli saw that the Arabs would lose their grip on things, given all the threats that the Africans were making against us, so he returned to the city of Ibra in Oman in 1961 and left us suffering with our indecisiveness until the inevitable day arrived.

I will never forget Sunday, January 12, 1964. The station "Sawt Zanzibar, The Voice of Zanzibar" broadcast the news about the coup and the departure of Sultan Sayyid Jamshid bin Abdullah Al Said from his palace, known as "Bayt al-Sahil, the coastal house." He fled to the naval port of Zanzibar with his family and entourage. He had boarded the Omani royal ship named "Sayyid Khalifa," not knowing exactly where he was going. All he knew was that he had to leave. Not only did he have to step down from the throne, but he had to leave the country too—he who hadn't been in office for more than 31 days. He was a simple man who loved to have a good time and enjoyed mingling with the public. That day wasn't a normal day in the history of Zanzibar, for the rumors that had been circulating among people in hushed whispers, about the Africans plotting something in collaboration with Julius Nyerere in Dar al-Salam, had been confirmed. People heard

through the Sawt Zanzibar station that the Africans had staged a coup
against Sultan Jamshid. People exchanged news, and rumors escalated
regarding the fate of the Sultan because many had been ignoring all the
stories and signs that pointed to his fate.

My father took me by hand to the house of the Omani sheikh Hamad
bin Salem al-Rawahi. He had been hosting a large number of Omanis.
Fear rose among us, as people exchanged stories of death and violence.
I was worried about Bi Soura, about the fate of my unborn child.
Sheikh al-Rawahi took out a pen and wrote on the façade of his house
in English that he was a pacifist. He drew the logo of a flame with a
piece of coal, and when the violent clashes increased, Sheikh al-Rawahi
asked the men to seek refuge in safe places and leave the women and
children at his house.

There was a situation where I actually saw a tear escape from the
eye of my strict father. It was when we heard that some Africans had
cut off the penis of Suleiman al-Sikiti, deputy of the police commis-
sioner. They had stuffed it into his mouth in front of his wife, before
brutally killing him. There were other stories, too, that led us to break
down and cry like women. All things Arab were being targeted, and
Omanis were being killed in brutal massacres. Women were raped,
and the pregnant among them were bayoneted in the bellies. That
day, many of us escaped by sea to Mombasa and Tanga, while others
went into hiding.

My father and I hid under a large Yusuf Effendi mandarin tree,
one whose leaves you may have been able to count but whose fruit could
not be counted at all. My father forbade me from eating the mandarins
because they were supposedly harmful. That was a common belief
among Africans in Zanzibar, and that's why my father had chosen that
tree for us to hide under.

We remained in hiding for three days. Sheikh al-Rawahi's maid would bring us food three times a day. We ate and slept under the Youssef Effendi tree. We took care of our bathroom needs nearby. Later, Sheikh al-Rawahi called for us, so we came out. He said, "We're going back to Oman." My heart sank.

On Sawt of Zanzibar station, those behind the coup said things that surprised us all. I remember them saying, "On this glorious day, our freedom has returned to us, as we free ourselves from the rule of the Wamanga colonists who have perched on our chest for decades and sold our grandparents and fathers as slaves." The revolutionaries had issued rulings via the station that Arabs were banned from leaving or entering Zanzibar for fear of a counter-revolution.

Some friends told me that Britain was using the greed of Nyerere, Tanganyika's president, promising the annexation of Tanzania and providing him with the resources and money necessary to wreak all this havoc on us. My father said that we would leave and never come back here again. I got down on my knees and begged him.

"Father, please I want to take Bi Soura and my son with us."

My father argued that we didn't have any passports or exit permits. After a few days of waiting and anxiety, I was surprised by my father's change of heart. He told me it was important to wait until his grandson was born while he worked on finding a way to get us out of there.

I promised Bi Soura to bring her to Oman to live with me as soon as our first child was born. Bi Soura was delighted. Her family didn't care anymore now that the rules of the game were reversed.

She gave birth to our first baby. I was by her side despite all the turmoil that pervaded the country. I shared with her those difficult moments although her mother shooed me away more than once.

Bi Soura's mother split the leso into two halves. She dressed the baby in one half and swaddled him with the other before putting him on the chest of Bi Soura, who couldn't stop crying. She breastfed him for the first time. We had agreed to call him "Amer," the prosperous, like the love that prospered between us. I took him from her lap. I said, "I'll take him to my father, maybe his heart will soften." I kissed her forehead, promising to bring him back shortly. She trusted me. She believed me, and I took off with him.

My father inspected him between his hands as he would inspect the fruit at the shamba. His face contorted with anger.

He said, "This one is mixed."

Silence fell between us. I wanted him to accept me, my marriage, and my son. But that seemed impossible.

"We'll travel. Me, you, and the little one," he said.

A thousand words got stuck in my throat, but I didn't say anything. I froze in my place. My father waved a document in his right hand.

"Look," he said. "I bought this document. An exit-no return document. I bought it from the aides of the sly Karoumi. You either leave with me, or you stay in this mess."

Zanzibar, "the land of zunuuj," was no longer a safe place for Arabs. You either had to save yourself or walk to your death on your own legs. I wasn't sure if my mother and aunts would accept Bi Soura or if they would look at her as one of Zanjal's children, a second-class Omani citizen. I wracked my brain for ideas, but even the best-case scenarios were very sour.

I had entered Africa against my will, and I was leaving it against my will. I carried Amer without one word of goodbye to Bi Soura, and

I never went back to her. I left, and all I had of her was a piece of leso draped over the body of our child and the last pale smile she planted on my face.

Aboard the ship from Zanzibar to Oman, there was nothing that could stop Amer's hunger and quiet his constant crying, so three women felt pity for him and suggested taking turns breastfeeding him and taking care of him until we arrived in Oman.

We came back in the mid-60s. The difference between Oman and Zanzibar was huge. All we found was an extension of the desert. There were no houses like the ones we had gotten used to seeing in Zanzibar. There were no bathrooms and no beds. No schools and no hospitals. Life was wretched. Not much had changed during the sixteen years I was gone with my father.

The people from my village in Samael nicknamed me "Hamdan the Swahili." With time, the nickname became a part of me. My father called Amer "son of Bi Soura." And with time, that nickname became a part of him.

Exhausted, I shut my eyes. I returned Amer's novel to its folder. I covered my body with a thick blanket, as the air conditioner blasted cold air on me. I imagined Bi Soura. I imagined the magnitude of her misery as Amer was growing up in a different part of the world, without her seeing him, without her receiving a letter that would reassure her heart. Without knowing for certain whether her son was dead or alive, and without seeing her first love. That's what geography and travel and chasing a morsel of livelihood do to us . . . I spiraled into sleep without permission.

TWVE

I DREAM OF the footsteps of a woman. I can't see her face or upper body. She climbs up the stairs from the lower to the upper level, running, the echo of her footsteps reverberating throughout the entire house. Her breathing grows louder, her pulse quickens. Her feet are bare. Her long dress is draped over her running legs, exposing them at times and concealing them at others. She reaches the upper floor. Her arms collide with the air. Then, she charges towards the rail of the balcony with all the speed she can muster.

I jumped out of bed. I caught my breath. Sweat oozed, hot, from my entire body. Cold drool touched my cheek at the edge of the pillow. I jumped up. I found myself surrounded by terrifying darkness. I turned on the lamp. I warded off the devil over and over again. But the fear wouldn't leave my heart!

Oh my God, I had seen Faneesh's dream. Unbelievable. The dream was exactly as Faneesh had described it. I kept my eyes open. I tried to process what had happened to me. I lay back, propping my back firmly against the pillows. It must have happened because I was anxious. Because I had allowed Faneesh's ideas to be transmitted to me. Because I had left the door of the "square" ajar. Damn it. What time was it now? I looked for the clock and found my phone nearby. Three a.m. "Damn this deplorable woman." I got out of bed. I drew the curtains back with my trembling hand. No corpse below. I calmed down. My breathing, which rose and fell in my chest, terrified me. I could barely hear anything else. I locked the door of my room with a key. I tried to go back to sleep. Tossing and turning, all I could see were those feet. Oh my. I couldn't remember what color they were. Were they actually women's feet? Were her toenails painted, or did she go natural? Did she clip her toenails well? I walked around the room. Questions gnawed at me. I was trying to remember something important. Did the woman actually throw her body off the balcony or was she just trying to . . . ?

I approached the tea shelf, as Amer referred to it. I put a Lipton bag and two spoonfuls of sugar in a cup, while the hot water danced around in the electric kettle. The tea was ready. I opened the door to the balcony and sat on the swing that Amer liked to sit on. The swing was dusty. As soon as that deplorable Faneesh had become certain that Amer wasn't going to sit on it, she neglected its daily cleaning. I put a clean towel on the swing and sat down. I drank the tea as I watched the sunrise. The voice of the muezzin reverberated from somewhere. He was followed by another muezzin. It had been a long time since I had last prayed. I quit praying ever since I realized that God had no need for the prayers that I performed out of courtesy for my father, the imam of the masjid. I quit praying ever since I realized that God had no need for my prayers, prayers that my mother used to gloat about in front of her neighbors. She would say, "My children never miss any of their daily prayers." The nostalgia for prayer suddenly tickled me. Perhaps I would feel

HUDA HAMED

some relief. I performed my ablutions and prayed peacefully. The verses flowed slowly, washing my heart of fear. I prayed like I had never stopped praying for a day in my life.

I went down to the kitchen early. Faneesh was surprised when she first saw me. She repeated aloud, "Bismillah, in the name of Allah." She was making coffee. The smell of the coffee spread everywhere. I craved a cup of coffee with her. I resisted my desire. I sat on a kitchen chair. I called for her. She poured some coffee in the big mug designated for her. She put it aside and sat across from me directly, a rectangular table between us.

"Faneesh, can you tell me all about your dream? Will you describe it for me thoroughly?"

She was even more surprised. Her eyes almost popped out of her face.

"Madame," she said. "I need this job. I don't want to lose it because of a dream."

"It's OK, Faneesh," I said. "I changed my mind. I want to hear you out now."

"Madame, believe me. I'll forget all about it as soon as possible."

"Tell me, Faneesh," I said. "Were they a white woman's or a black woman's feet?"

"I can't remember," she said. "I can't remember. All I know is that that they were the feet of a woman."

"How did you know for sure that they were a woman's feet?" I asked. "Did she take care of her toenails? Were they painted for example?"

"No. I mean, I'm not sure. I think she had soft feet," she said. "They looked like women's feet to me."

"Faneesh. Try to remember," I said. "Did the woman actually jump over the balcony rail or was she intending to jump?"

"Madame, I'm not sure. The dream makes me dizzy. I feel confused after I wake up."

"I understand."

"Madame, would you like some coffee?"

I don't know what happened to me. I took the cup of coffee from her hand. I couldn't resist the smell. It tasted great too. She kept watching me as I took a few sips from the cup, as if she couldn't believe what she was seeing.

"Madame, I brought this coffee with me from Addis Ababa so I can remember my family and the fields where my father works."

I didn't say anything. I felt like I couldn't recognize myself as I was getting dragged into details that I had no business getting into. Here she was leaving the "square" with my consent and all because of a damn dream. I took the coffee upstairs. I contemplated the mural, its little stories dispersed here and there. I grabbed a big brush, bigger than the usual one, and some acrylic paint. I tried painting the feet. My memory was being stingy with the details. I drew the two feet, and two legs. A dress draped over the legs. What color was the dress? I wasn't certain. I proposed that the dress be black. I groomed her toenails. There was no need for nail polish. The skin on the back of her feet was rough. I imagined it to be a little rough. Faneesh's scream jolted me out of the mural that I was now immersed in. I turned to her.

"Madame," she said. "These feet look just like the feet of the suicidal woman. I just remembered something now."

"What, Faneesh?"

"She was wearing something over her right ankle. Something that made a sound."

"Aha. Something like a bangle?" I said. "What did it look like? What color was it?"

"I don't remember exactly," she said. "It made a sound. I heard two sounds, the sound of her breathing and the sound of something jingling on her right foot."

I drew on the right foot a dainty silver-colored bangle. I darkened the color of the feet. They appeared as a light bronze color. The feet were not on the same level. One rose while the other fell. The tip of the black dress rose on one side and unfolded on the other. I took a look at the feet from a distance. I could almost feel their movement. I noticed that Faneesh was still there. She was looking at the painting with surprise, as if saying, "How did you do that, Madame? How did you get inside my head?" The feet gave the mural a special luster, despite looking a little deviant. Faneesh collected my brushes and coloring tools. She put things back in their place.

Faneesh must have thought that the dream and mural could open doors for conversation between us. I washed my hands thoroughly in the bathroom. I applied sanitizer. The doorbell rang. It had been a long time since anyone had come knocking at our door. Faneesh opened the door. Tarfa hugged and kissed me. She sat down, in all her playfulness and mischief, and started asking how I was doing. She asked about Raya, Yusuf and Amer. She bombarded me with questions. She told me all about her good news. About the last abaya that I designed for her that wowed the women who'd attended the wedding at the Nour Hall in the city of Sultan Qaboos. She said she'd given my business card to every woman who asked about the design of the abaya and the drawings on the sheilah. We moved from one story to another. From one piece of gossip to another. Then she suddenly seemed to notice something about me.

"You look tired."

"I didn't sleep well."

"Please don't tell me it's because of the maid's dream."

"This time it was because of *my* dream."

"*Your* dream?"

I told her about the contagion. The way the dream had been transmitted to me.

Tarfa thought for a little bit and then said, "It happened because you were thinking about it, because the whole thing took over your mind. The transmission of the dream sounds like a fantasy, Zahiyya."

I stopped talking. Faneesh brought some fresh orange juice along with some cookies and nuts. She served us and left.

"Zahiyya," Tarfa said. "Faneesh is a good maid. You won't find someone like her."

"The situation is now bigger than me and her. What if there was a suicidal woman in my house?"

"You were the first to build and live in the house."

"Well, if this weren't about some woman's past, could it be about some woman's future?"

"Zahiyya," she said. "Get these silly thoughts out of your head."

We stopped talking. We didn't have anything else to say to each other. Tarfa sipped her juice.

"Your maid is from Africa," she said. "You better watch out."

"I don't understand," I said.

"I mean, she might do something to you."

"Ok, what am I going to do?"

"You have two options. Either you fire her, or you make her understand."

"Make her understand?"

"I mean, you should give her some space to talk and vent."

Tarfa was trying to make me understand her own experience. She told me that establishing a friendship with the maid is the best way to gain her affection. She would tell her maids on their first day, "You're not maids. You're members of the family." Tarfa would tell herself that lie, which she actually believed. She did that because her son Sami was too young to go to school. She feared that someone might hurt him while she was gone at work. But I had nothing to fear, except for the blessing of cleanliness. Yusuf and Raya grew up in my lap, and I rarely allowed maids to even touch them. I prepared their food and fed them myself. I ran their baths for them. I took them on outings. I dropped them off at school and brought them back. The maids viewed Raya and Yusuf as something sacred. Something untouchable. That's why I was never forced to bow down to maids. I was never forced to plead for their affection. My mother—whose spine was bent because of multiple pregnancies and work and chasing her kids—was right about one thing, which she said every time a new maid came to our house. "To need a maid's help is to be humiliated by her hands!" This sentence sums up our relationship with them.

Tarfa changed the subject and started talking about other things. About the new beauty salon that opened near my house.

About the Filipina girls who could remove facial hair with swift movements. "Take a look, Zahiyya," she said. "They cleaned up my entire face so well. It wasn't painful. The new Filipina woman had such a light touch. She even gave me a facial. A fruit facial. I feel so good. Like a new woman."

I don't go to beauty salons. The only time I ever went to a beauty salon was the night of my wedding. I don't like the idea of Asian women spying on my body. I pluck my own eyebrows in the bathroom. As soon as a hair grows, I'm there to ambush it. I wax my upper lip and chin weekly. Amer couldn't believe it when he saw my picture in junior high. My moustache was so conspicuous. My mother told me, "No waxing of the moustache before you're married. No plucking of the eyebrows because God has damned the plucker and the plucked." I was very hairy. My Omani roommate in Egypt was so skilled. She would prepare a sugar paste wax in the kitchen and sit down in her short skirt in the living room. She would spread the wax across her legs, adhere to it a piece of cloth, and pull it off without even uttering an "ouch," as she watched black-and-white films starring Rushdi Abaza and Suad Husni. I asked her to make a sugar paste wax for me. I watched her. Fattoum asked me if I wanted her to remove the hair on my arms and legs. Winking, she gestured with her eyes towards my armpits as well. I froze in my place. I took the wax to my room and spread it over my legs, but every time I tried to pull it off my skin, I groaned and moaned from pain. My movements grew slower. I wondered to myself how come Fattoum could wax her legs, with her eyes fixed on Rushdi Abaza. It was as if it wasn't her own leg. She would spread around the wax and then pull it at an amazing pace. I was determined to keep going. My heart beat faster. I repressed my screams every time I watched a forest of black hair disappear off my body. Deep breath. One, two, three, and pull. That was followed by a long exhale. I did it again. Deep breath. I was getting faster at it. I won't lie and say that the pain subsided with time. Truth is, I was getting used to the pain. When I stood on the bed in front of the mirror and looked at my legs under the short skirt, I felt like I was Faten Hamama. However, I was chubbier and darker than her. I tried to dance like Hind Rustum, but my body wouldn't work with me. I was a stiff woman. I flopped on the bed. I lifted one leg and lowered the other, alternating. Before going to sleep, I told myself, "There are two kinds of pain. There's the kind of pain that my father plants on my back, the one that turns green, swells up, and then turns into blue, leaving a scar in my heart. And then there's the pain that harvests black forests and gives me legs that are fit for a legendary woman."

Tarfa left. Clamor left with her. Tarfa possessed a ringing laugh and an endless supply of gossip that never got dull. She was the perfect fruit that brightened up trips and evenings. Scrumptious through thick and thin.

I went into the kitchen to prepare my lunch. I always made my own meals. Faneesh made her own meals in the same kitchen, using the same stove. But we only exchanged the smells of our different dishes. Faneesh looked at me. The curiosity in her eyes bothered me. She turned her attention away from me. I noticed that she was sprinkling something over her small pieces of beef. It had a white, greenish color.

"What's that, Faneesh?"

"It's sanafik, Madame."

"Sanafik?"

"It's a very hot spice mix," she said. "I brought it with me from Ethiopia. I must have it in my food."

She put the undercooked meat cubes on her plate. Then she placed some strange-looking bread next to the plate. It was the first time I had ever paid attention to her food. It looked so unusual.

"Faneesh, aren't you going to put the meat in the oven?" I asked.

"No, I'm going to eat it raw."

I gasped out loud . . . Did she really say that?

She smiled, and her face lit up. "I'm making the Ethiopian dish fourt, Madame. It's made with raw meat. That's how we eat it."

"Raw? That's disgusting!"

"Madame," she said. "This was a favorite meal among Ethiopian emperors and kings. I also baked some injera this morning. In my family, we eat this tasty bread daily."

I went back to preparing my cut of beef. I checked more than once to make sure that the meat I was preparing for myself was sufficiently cooked. I was going to eat it with Lebanese bread and a big bowl of salad. Faneesh's appetite for talking must not grow larger. Otherwise, my own troubles would grow alongside it.

"Madame, would you like to taste from my dish and I'll taste from yours?" she asked. "Yours also looks really tasty!"

The world around me started to spin. This woman's rudeness and boldness were increasing, day after day. I was the reason. I didn't respond to her stupid suggestion. My sharp look said it all. I turned off the stove as soon as I noticed that my food was ready.

I made myself a plate. I left some of my food in the pot for her so I wouldn't seem like a merciless, heartless woman. I left the kitchen. I sat in the living room flipping through the channels and eating my lunch until I got sleepy. I called for her to take away the dishes and wash them. Then I went to my room to sleep.

I dream of the woman's footsteps as she climbs from the bottom floor to the upper floor. Her breathing grows louder, and her pulse quickens as if it is right next to my ear. Her feet are bare. Her long black dress is draped over her running legs, exposing them at times and concealing them at others. She reaches the upper floor. Her arms collide with the air. I notice her feet. They are not smooth. The toenails aren't clipped. But they are clean. I confirm that there is a bangle on her right ankle. Then, with all the speed she can muster, she charges in the direction of the balcony rail.

I jumped out of bed. I caught my breath. This all happened in less than five minutes . . . Oh, my God! It was the dream, again. Who was that woman, walking with her own legs toward death? Why did she want to die in my house? My body was exhausted, craving sleep. My brain was scattered. I hurried down to the kitchen. I took the stairs that the suicidal woman had been climbing a little while earlier. I entered the kitchen. Faneesh was busy washing the dishes. She glanced at me again. Terrified of the sound of my footsteps, she repeated, "Bismillah, in the name of Allah."

"Faneesh, did you have the dream again?"

"No, madame," she said. "The dream stopped coming to me a few days ago. Alhamdulillah, thank God."

"How many times have you had this dream?"

"I don't remember. Every time I put my head down, I had the dream."

I sat down on a chair in the kitchen. Worried, at a loss. I didn't have the ability to draw or to go back to reading Ammi Hamdan's journal. I couldn't tell Faneesh what was happening to me. I wasn't going to break the barriers between us because of a dream. Maybe I needed to tell Amer what was happening. But he would worry. I didn't want him to worry.

"Madame, thank you for leaving me some of your food," she said. "That's very sweet of you. It was so delicious. I've always wanted to taste your food."

I wanted to get up on my feet. My strength failed me. The world began to spin. I fell to the floor.

THIR13EEN

I WOKE UP. Faneesh was standing over my head. She was clearly worried. I suddenly found myself in my room, in my bed. How had Faneesh carried me upstairs?

"Madame, are you OK?" she asked. "Should I call Mr. Amer or one of your girlfriends?"

"There's no need for that. I'm OK."

I lifted my back, propping myself up on the pillows that Faneesh helped stack behind me.

"You should see a doctor."

"I don't want to see anyone," I said. "Get back to work."

"Madame, if you need anything, just give me a call on my phone," she said. "I'll come immediately."

Faneesh left. She had placed some lemon juice with mint at my bedside. She was trying hard to save her job—if only it were not for some of her inappropriate intrusions. The phone rang. It was Amer calling. I felt a serious desire to cry. I gulped. I decided not to tell him anything. He would worry. His listless, tired voice reached me.

"Zahiyya, I couldn't find anything that would lead me to my mother," he said. "All I know are her first and last name. A simple physical description of her. I was told that many African women married Omanis. I heard many stories. Someone told me that her family may have fled to England and gotten English citizenship, but there's no confirmation of that story. Another person told me that she got married and moved to Burundi. They said that some of her family members fled, that some were imprisoned, and that some died during the coup. I worry about my father Hamdan. These stories would depress him."

"Habibi, my darling, you've done what you can. Don't be upset."

"Zahiyya, I'm happy to be in this spot where my parents met," he said. "I feel happy because I can now fill in all the missing details in my novel. I am looking for a story. But my father is looking for Bi Soura."

"Inshallah, God willing, we'll figure out something that we can tell Ammi Hamdan."

"I'll stay here for a few more days. Maybe some new information will turn up."

Amer's tone changed a little bit. He seemed more optimistic. He told me about having ugali, a dish made with sweet corn that he had mentioned in his novel but hadn't tasted before. There were many things that Amer had written about in his novel based on Ammi Hamdan's memory, and now he was experiencing them in person.

I didn't tell him anything about my dream or illness. I didn't want him to worry. I assured him that everything was fine and ended the phone call. I was so weak, I could neither get up nor go to sleep. The minutes passed slowly in the room. There was no one with me, except for the ghost of a woman planning her death. Boredom gnawed at me, but I knew that if I called Tarfa or Hind, the story would get bigger and juicier. Who could I open up to about this secret? So far, Tarfa knew half the secret. If Tarfa were to know that the dream was recurrent, she'd think that I was hallucinating. She might tell me to see a doctor. Or, she might say that God was punishing me for the inhumane ways I've treated maids. She would find plenty of things to say. It would be best if the secret never left my mouth. I don't know why I suddenly remembered the story of the barber that I used to tell Raya and Yusuf. It was about a prince with long ears and a barber whose chest tightened up with the prince's secret. Just as my chest tightened up with the dream of the suicidal woman.

I didn't have the energy to lift my weak body since I hadn't slept well. Every time I tried to get up, I felt dizzy. I didn't want the story to get out of control among my friends Hind and Tarfa, and I didn't want to become a laughingstock. I also didn't feel like telling Amer for fear that he would get more worried about me. I didn't have the energy to prepare a light meal that would tide me over. I resisted my exhaustion by propping my back against some pillows so I could sit up. I noticed a light knock at the door. Faneesh entered before I gave her permission to come in. With a pleasant smile, she said good morning and drew the window curtains aside. The light pierced my eyes.

"Good morning, Madame," she said.

She put a tray of food on a small table that she set over my stretched legs.

"You need to eat so you can get strong, Madame."

I noticed the food she'd put in front of me. I was about to throw it in her face.

"What's this?" I asked. "Take it away."

She pushed the tray closer to me.

"Madame, this is tadej, or taj," she said. "It's a famous drink in Ethiopia. It's basically made up of white honey and water, fermented together. It's very tasty, and it's good for you. And this is coffee with milk. It's very tasty too. Just try it. We call it bunna in Amharic. And these are injera bread pieces that I put some meat on top. And this is orange juice and boiled eggs."

"Take this nasty food out of here and make me a normal breakfast."

Faneesh stood there. "You never taught me how to make the food you like," she said boldly. "So I will make you the food that I know how to make." She withdrew leaving the tray in its place.

Hunger pains stabbed at me. I drank the orange juice and had the egg. Then, I don't know how my hand found the courage to grab a piece of injera bread. It was tasty, but I was too scared to eat the meat that sat on top of it. I took a few sips from the taj drink, as she called it. It wasn't bad. It tasted acceptable to me since I am a fan of honey. As soon as I was done, I felt a little embarrassed. I was so weak and needed help! Faneesh came in. Her face lit up when she saw that I had tried everything she'd prepared.

"You'll regain your strength quickly, Madame," she said, her tone like that of someone feeling the joy of victory.

As soon as she had uttered that sentence, I felt a serious urge to throw up. I tried to repress the urge and then burst like a balloon. I emptied everything in my stomach onto my clothes and bed. Faneesh rushed to help me. I asked her to leave me alone. I tried to kick her out of the room three times. I didn't like for anyone to see me weak like that. But she opened the closet and picked out some clean pajamas for me—the first pair that her eyes fell upon. She grabbed a washcloth from the upper shelf and put it next to the pajamas on the hanger. Then she wrapped my right arm around her left shoulder and pulled me to her, ignoring my screams. She left me near the toilet bowl so I could finish throwing up whatever was left in my stomach.

She helped me take my dirty clothes off. My tears were so close then. My tears were close but didn't trickle down my face, and Faneesh didn't notice them. Standing in front of her in my underwear, I felt like someone walking naked in a city crowded with people. She helped me put on the clean pajamas without looking at me. She kept holding me as I rinsed my face and mouth. She handed me the sanitizer so I could wipe my hands. She laid my body down on a chair and stripped the bed. She brought fresh bedding from the linen closet. She made my bed and then lifted me up to it, propping many pillows behind my back. She opened the window to air out the room and then sprayed some air freshener. She patted my hands as she covered me with a blanket. I didn't know if I should thank her, so I decided to stay quiet. I closed my eyes and quickly dozed off.

She leaps up the stairs in my house. The woman is wearing a dress with a black bottom, with green circles that look like very small green flowers. I try hard to see her face, but I can't get any additional details. She quickens her pace on the stairs. Her breathing grows louder. The echo of her footsteps reverberates in the empty house like music from a horror movie. I realize that my house is now empty, with no furniture. It looks like the house Amer and I had first walked into—empty except for the whiteness of its walls. She reaches the upper floor. Her pace slows. She gets to the living room right across from the balcony. She injects her panting body with some renewed energy. She runs towards the balcony.

I fell off the bed. My body hit the cold tiles. I was terrified by the amount of drool that flowed out of my mouth. I was terrified by the trembling of my body and its feverishness. I pulled my body back up onto the bed. I wrapped myself with the blanket. I felt an overwhelming desire to cry. What was happening to me now? Who was this woman? Why did she want to commit suicide in my home? Did she really commit suicide? Or was she still thinking about it, and for how long was she going to chase me? What did she want from me? What?

Faneesh knocked on the door and entered before I gave her permission to come in. She put her hand on my forehead.

"Your temperature is still high, Madame," she said. "Is there something I can do for you?"

"No."

"Madame, should I call someone?" she asked. "I'm worried about you."

"I said no."

"OK, I'll be in my room if you need anything."

"What are you doing in your room?"

"Madame, I got all my work done."

"I mean what do you usually do during your free time?"

I don't know why I had asked her that question. Maybe I was taking Tarfa's advice about the importance of creating a space for conversation between us. Or maybe I was afraid that the suicidal woman was going to come out of somewhere. Faneesh sat at the edge of my rug. I felt an itch in my body. I repressed my rage.

"Madame, I like reading."

"Aha, that's why Mr. Amer gave you stories to read."

Her color changed. Her face was flushed.

"When Mr. Amer found out that I had completed my freshman year in English literature, he worried that I might forget the language, or reading, during my years of service, so he gave me some books that were Raya's and Yusuf's. I'm always reading so I don't forget. I write as well."

"What do you write?" I asked. "Please don't tell me you write novels, Faneesh."

"No, Madame. I wouldn't go that far. I am writing my personal memoirs."

"You mean you write about everything? Even the people you work with?"

"I write about some situations and stories. And, of course I write about people who pass through my life."

I had a terrible feeling then. That woman was writing about me. Who knows? Maybe she had turned me into some juicy material for her stupid stories. She might have portrayed me as an evil, cold-hearted woman, while depicting Amer as a chivalrous, noble gentleman. Who knows? Maybe she thought that Amer was giving her books because he loved her? Maybe she was writing her memoirs to show that she can write well, just like Amer! Damn you, deplorable woman. Here I was, suffering the fever of a wretched dream while being written into the memoirs of my maid without her asking for my permission.

Faneesh left the room cheerful, beaming with happiness because a wall had collapsed between us. I picked up the phone and called my friend Hind. Hind was nothing like Tarfa. She was calm and straightlaced. She was the same age as we were, but she thought like a mother or grandmother. My sick, tired voice surprised her. My nonstop crying and inability to say anything coherent surprised her.

"I'll be there in the time it takes me to drive."

Forty-five minutes later, I was in her lap. She looked at me, surprised. My pale face, my short, disheveled hair. The room reeked of the odors of sickness and painkillers, despite having been aired and scrubbed.

Hind took me by the hand to the balcony where the breeze was gentle. It was afternoon. We sat on the green swing and rocked a little. We watched the passersby. They seemed very small from the upper floor. Hind asked me to talk since talking might ease some of my worries. I wasn't exactly certain of what she was saying. She asked me if Amer's and the children's absence was doing all this to me. Maybe yes. Their absence . . . there were other reasons too. I wouldn't know where to start, Hind. There was a lot to talk about, and talking was exhausting. The story seemed so fantastical! If anyone else had told it to me, I would have laughed and laughed until I fell down.

"Hind, what would you think of a maid who writes her memoirs? Of someone writing about you and your husband and children?" I asked.

I found myself telling her everything. Lightening the burden of my fears. I told her the story from the beginning. I told her about the contagion of the dream and about the sleep that fled from me. I told her about Faneesh who was writing and who was controlling me like a puppet with the strings of her stories.

"Oh God . . . it's a scary story, Zahiyya."

"See what I mean? That's it. I'm thinking of kicking her out of my house," I said. "Maybe if I kick her out, I'll be at peace. She came here and brought trouble with her. But I'm worried that Amer might say that I have a complex. You know how Amer thinks."

"No, no . . . don't kick her out," she said. "She might do something to you. All you've done is eat her food, and look what happened to you. Imagine what would happen if you fired her."

"OK, what should I do?"

"Listen, habibti," she said. "This woman has cast a spell on you. I say go search her room."

"No, Hind. I don't believe these superstitions."

"Superstitions?" she asked. "Fine, let her mess with you until she drives you crazy."

Hind stood up. She adjusted the sheilah on her head and straightened out her abaya. She grabbed her purse and dangled it over her right shoulder. Faneesh met her with a glass of orange juice and a rehearsed smile, but Hind walked past her as if she hadn't even seen her.

I regretted telling her that story. I leaned on the railing of the balcony. It was from here that the woman threw herself every night. I looked down. There was no trace of a corpse. I thought about the fate of a body that jumped from this height. Survival seemed impossible or perhaps possible but with many broken bones.

I felt dizzy, so I left the balcony in order to drive the dream out of my head. I turned around, and I was faced by the feet that I had drawn on the mural across from the balcony. One foot was climbing while the other beat it by a step. At that moment, I discovered an irony that I had not planned. The feet were exactly across from the balcony. I felt the desire to do something, and I started drawing from the bottom upwards. I drew an extension to the black dress. The woman became larger than me. Taller than me. I brought the small ladder that I usually used when working on the wall. I climbed the ladder. I kept climbing, and the woman's body got taller and taller. I cinched her dress at the waist. By that time, I was halfway up the wall. I found myself panting behind her. I was breathing in an abnormal way. Her right hand was raised, almost touching her chest. Her left arm extended far behind her. I added some effects so the woman would seem like she was running, tired. I was running with her. I was drawing the outline of this woman I didn't know. Her chest protruded in front of her, as if she had just taken a deep breath that she had not yet exhaled. Her shoulders were strong. She appeared to be in her forties, about my age, or maybe a little younger. But she was taller and skinnier than me. I drew for her a long, beautiful neck at the end of the ceiling, and then I stopped suddenly. I took a step back so I could see her. She was twice my height. I couldn't fill in the colors of her dress. I just drew its outline. Every time I looked at her, I became certain that she was running towards me. For a second, I felt as if she was going to walk over my body, trample me as she headed for the destination she desired. She looked scary as she ran, her head cut off.

I was startled by the sound of the laundry basket that dropped from Faneesh's hands. She was carrying it up to the roof where the clothesline was. I glanced at her. She was staring at the running woman. Then she burst out crying. She cried in a loud voice, as she trembled with fear. I ran toward the balcony door and closed

HUDA HAMED

it so her crying wouldn't reach the neighbors' ears. I extended my arm to touch her shoulder after some hesitation and asked her cautiously, "Faneesh, what is it?"

"Tell me, Madame," she said. "Has this woman been visiting you in your dreams?"

I couldn't come up with a good answer. When I grabbed her by the shoulders and told her to stop, she threw herself in my bosom and hugged me. I felt goose bumps eating at my body. Her sticky, sweaty body made me dizzy. I pushed her away from me.

"Faneesh, stop. I said stop!"

"You know her, right?" she said. "This woman lives here among us. I was happy that she had stopped coming to me in a dream. Here she is now, growing bigger on the wall."

"Faneesh, calm down."

But she kept holding on to me as I looked at the running woman for an instant and at Faneesh in another.

We went downstairs. We sat at the kitchen table together. It was not an easy decision for me to tell her, but she was the only person who could understand what I was going through now. She made Ethiopian coffee for us. She handed me a cup while she gulped her cup of coffee with extraordinary speed.

"Yes, Faneesh. The suicidal woman, running, has been visiting me in a dream for a few days now, and I don't know how to get rid of her except by painting her."

"So you drew her across from the balcony in order to fulfill her wish?"

"That didn't occur to me."

"Why is she without a head?"

"I don't know. I don't know if I'm going to draw a head for her or not."

"If you draw one, it will be drooping from the ceiling, like she was hanged."

"Why are you saying that?"

"Haven't you noticed that you've drawn the neck at the farthest point on the wall?"

"Forget about the mural for now," I said. "Tell me, when did the woman disappear from your dreams?"

"As far as I remember, it was when I talked to you about her and divulged the secret I had been keeping to myself . . . What if you tell someone else about her? Maybe she would leave your dreams too."

"So the contagion can spread to the person I tell?"

We both stopped talking. I kept sipping my coffee without looking at her.

"Madame, are you hungry?"

"Very."

"How about I make for you some anitcha?" she said. "It's a lamb stew with onions, garlic, tomatoes, and butter. It's very tasty. I won't put too much hot sauce."

"No, please!" I said "I'm craving some meat kabsa. I'll make it myself."

"Madame, please teach me how to make it," she said. "Let me make you the food you like."

"OK, Faneesh," I said. "I'm going to give you the opportunity of your lifetime. I'm going to teach you how to prepare this dish."

Faneesh fluttered with happiness. She jumped from her seat, light as a feather. She took out the lamb stew meat and put it in warm water to thaw. She chopped up three onions and three cloves of garlic. I started sautéing them with some Omani ghee and taught her how to season the meat according to some secret steps that require a lot of meticulousness, especially since I don't use measuring cups but rather follow my instincts.

A little cardamom and some cloves and cinnamon sticks, then a few bay leaves to bring about that special smell. Faneesh asked me about the green pepper, so I told her to put it over the mixture that was now turning a little red and to add the tomatoes and a sprinkle of saffron. I added other spices like black pepper and cumin and coriander, as Faneesh took notes while I talked to her about what it means for someone to have "nafas," a "breath" for cooking. I put the meat over the mixture so that it could absorb all the tasty flavors. I added hot water with dried lemon pieces. I left the meat until it was cooked, and then put it in the oven to brown it. Then I added the rice to the seasoned meat broth.

Our first collaborative dish came out. Faneesh cleaned the kitchen, washed all the dishes that I'd used, and cleaned the containers of the special spices with a wet rag before putting them back in their places. She washed her hands and then put some of the tasty meat kabsa on a plate for me before making a plate for herself. When I sat down to eat at the kitchen table, she asked for permission to go eat in the courtyard. Without thinking, I gestured to her to sit with me at the table.

"Thank you for your kindness, Madame," she said. "The food is amazing."

"Faneesh, are you saving some money?"

"Only a little bit since I send most of my monthly salary to my father."

"What about the rest? What are you going to do with it?" I asked. "The previous housekeepers who worked here had plans to find better opportunities, like getting married or building houses or sending their children to school. What about you?"

"I only have one dream," she said. "To go back to school and finish my degree so my parents won't need for anything. What about you, Madame? What do you dream of?"

I looked at us sitting next to each other at the same table. I contemplated her question; it confirmed to me that I was one of her memoirs' puppets and that anything I said now would end up in her stupid pages. I jumped up, and my chair fell.

"I'm the one who gets to ask the questions here. You just work here," I said. "If you cross the line again, I'll kick you out of my house. Got it?"

I went up to my room like a madwoman, as I thought about the running woman. Maybe she was carrying something that resembled my own anger, exhaustion, and questions. I slipped into bed and cried. I had a splitting headache.

It was my fifth day without regular sleep. I cried and cried until I was overcome with tiredness, and I saw myself again at the bottom of the stairs where I was a little while ago.

The running woman tightens the grip of her right hand over my left hand, forcing me to advance. I refuse and retreat, but her strong hand pulls me and makes me climb stairs that shrink under our feet. I hear her accelerating heartbeats, and I don't have the energy to lift my head so I can see her fully. I can only see up to her waist. Fear pulls my head downwards, where I see nothing but the stairs rushing under me. On the second floor, she pushes her right foot forward while the left foot goes backward. She presses harder on my fingers, and I feel as if she is about to break them, one finger at a time. She takes a deep breath and runs, still gripping my hand.

I screamed for a long time, before I finally woke up. The fingers on my left hand were swollen, as if the blood had been trapped in them for a while. My left hand seemed bigger than my right one.

I had no choice. I had to call Amer and tell him. His phone rang. His voice reached me, calm and happy. I controlled myself. He told me he found Ammi Hamdan's friend, the one who refused to move back to Oman, the one to whom Oman would remain a dream. He said, "My father's friend told me these never-ending stories, and he gave me back the writing appetite that I had lost ever since my father Hamdan started repeating the same old details about Bi Soura."

Amer was brimming with happiness, like someone whose dream had come true. I was happy for him. He was content with the simple joys that made his heart swell like a little boy who'd gotten a holiday cookie on Eid. I didn't want to dampen his good mood as he said, "I drowned, writing an entire chapter. That's why I haven't called you habibti." He also said he was going out with his father's friend and that he'd sent me the chapter by email and hoped that I would read it. I told him enthusiastically "I will" and that I was doing well and painting regularly and that life was all rosy. He blew me a virtual kiss, and the phone call ended with rushed words of love and longing.

FOU14EEN

THE CLOCK POINTED to seven in the evening. I felt as if I were hanging in space, and my head throbbed with pain. Two Panadols and I'd be fine. I went downstairs to the kitchen. I took out a piece of paper from the notebook in which I jotted down any groceries we needed. I wrote: bread, fresh milk, yoghurt, strawberries, zucchini, and eggplant. What else? I checked the freezer and resumed writing. Eggs, lettuce, and halloum cheese. Faneesh came in and seemed a little nervous when I looked her in the eye.

"I was taking out the trash, Madame."

"Here's a list of groceries. Wash your hands well and go to the nearby supermarket for grocery shopping. Can you do that?" I said. "I'm exhausted. I can't go with you today."

Faneesh nodded in agreement, happy. I gave her a fifty-riyal bill and asked her to bring back a receipt.

"Madame, can I buy some things for myself? With my own money, of course."

"You can do that," I said. "But don't be late."

Faneesh flew off like a homing pigeon loaded with letters. I now had my golden opportunity. It was the first time I ever allowed one of my maids to go to the market without my prying eyes accompanying her and overseeing the selection of fruits and vegetables. Oh, how many things had changed since that young woman had set foot in my house, and how many rules she'd broken! And here I was, thinking about going into her room and looking through her belongings, in search of the "spell" she was hiding somewhere. I had never once entered the maid's room in my entire life. Many had passed through it. The maid's room and bathroom are outside my house. I never believed that people could put a "spell" on others, even when Jokha had talked to me about it one day with so much pain, when we were alone. She talked about Bi Soura and the "spell" that she had put on Ammi Hamdan, which made him not see anyone but her, not utter the name of any woman but her, and turned him away from life and its joys.

Oh God. Could Faneesh have done the same thing with me? I almost believed that, for here she was today outside the "square," in the early months of her service, and here I was unable to make the decision to fire her.

I entered her room. I opened the box where Amer kept all the spare keys. I had marked the key to the maid's room by putting it on the keychain in the shape of a pair of shoes that Tarfa had bought me as a gift from Germany. I did that after the time we had to call the police and report that a strange male had entered our house and snuck into the Indonesian maid's room. It had taken over half an hour to go through all the keys, and by that time, her lover had gone out the back window. I hesitated, wondering whether what I was doing was permissible or not. I told myself that it was my house and that I had the right to enter all of its rooms without any exceptions.

I was surprised by how clean the room was. The floor was wiped clean. The bed was neat, and the blanket was folded with all the pillows propped up in the right places. I leaned and pulled out a few bags from under the bed. I opened all of them. The bags contained all the gifts that I had occasionally given her. I opened the closet. The uniforms were hanging next to one another, and down below, there were some folded jeans and cotton shirts. I didn't dare touch them. She had put her underwear in the drawers. They seemed worn out, their colors almost faded. Some of her bras were ripped, and she seemed to have sewn the different parts together with a needle. On the top shelf of the closet, there was a pair of old running shoes that she had been wearing when she came from the Ain office to Muscat. I closed the door to the closet. I hesitated a lot before opening the bathroom door. I opened it. The smell of detergent emanated from it, like the rest of my house. The window sparkled. The mirror was clean. The toothbrush leaned over a tube of Signal Two toothpaste in its own cup. The shampoo, hair conditioner, a comb, and a loofah gathered in a basket that hung on the wall. I had told Faneesh to get rid of that fruit basket after I'd bought a new one, so she put it to good use.

I darted my eyes in all directions in search of the hidden "spell," but I didn't know what I was looking for. What could that spell be? Was it a worn-out ragdoll, like the one we saw in movies, or was it a buried bag? Frankly, I didn't know what I was looking for. It could be something she was putting in my food or drink.

I was about to leave the room before Faneesh could come back, when a small table in the lobby caught my attention. A small, yellow journal with two protruding brown teddy bears sat on the table. The teddy bears kept looking at me as they hugged one another. Faneesh had placed a pen in the last third of the notebook. I opened the notebook to the last paragraph she'd written. "Madame Zahiyya is very sick. I am unable to help her." I panicked. I felt like a thief. I put the notebook back in its place. But curiosity came back and gnawed at me. What else had she written about me? What had she written about Amer? How did the logic of maids perceive me? My curiosity grew as I worried that she was going to be back any moment. Talking myself into it, I told myself, "What if this notebook was the spell? Really. She could have written the magic here with her pen, and as soon as I'd read the magic, it would dissolve." I put the yellow journal under my arm. I could feel the fear of the protruding bears as they hugged one another tightly. I locked the door to Faneesh's room. I went up to my room and locked the door. I peeled off some of my clothes and lay down in my bed in an undershirt and shorts. I caught my breath and opened the notebook to the first page. She had written her diaries in English, which forced me to resort to Google Translate on my cell phone. Faneesh began her memoirs with this short sentence: *"Because I'm so sad today, I've decided to start a journal so I could write in between its lines my good and bitter days before they slip from my hands."*

Faneesh had written her first lines on 01/07/2005, and based on a rudimentary calculation of her age, she must have been in her first year of college studying literature as she'd told us previously. On the next page, she wrote:

02/02/2005

My father asked me today to go with him to the coffee fields. I am in love with the coffee in whose fields I grew up in Addis Ababa. I love my color that is the same color as coffee. I hold up a coffee bean to my skin and find them very similar. It's as if the coffee bean is a part of me, or as if I'm a part of it.

I laughed. It was the first time I'd ever heard someone speak so proudly of the color black and see it as an extension of other relationships within the environment. On the next page, Faneesh drew a tree with a black pen. I thought it must be the coffee tree she'd talked about. I told myself: this drawing is extremely primitive. I kept on reading.

02/18/2005

Today, my friend Zanash, who is years older than me, brought me a book that she described as one of the most important books of the twentieth century in France. It was **The Little Prince**, by French author Antoine de Saint-Exupéry, translated into English. I will start reading it after I am done helping my father in the fields. Zanash works with the UNICEF organization that promotes girls' education, and she passes down to me some of the books written in English. I used to have so much difficulty reading them, but I would persist and go to her with questions sometimes. Then I'd come back with even more enthusiasm for reading during my rare free time.

My father was waiting for a son to help him in the coffee fields. I was the eldest, but I was a girl, so my father provided the funds for my education and school supplies when he sensed my passion for learning. I used to travel a tremendously long distance on foot to get to my school. I loved school and reading, but soon my father's financial situation took a turn for the worse, so he kept me at home after I'd completed my elementary education. He said that it was more important and useful for my brother Jerma to get an education instead. I felt depressed, but I survived by reading the books that were still available to me. I would read them and write down notes in the margins so I wouldn't forget what I'd learned. Whenever Jerma tossed his belongings and skipped school, I would sneak a look at his books and sometimes gather up the courage to do his homework. He conspired with me—he made good grades while I kept practicing and learning and did not stop helping my father in the coffee fields.

HUDA HAMED

At the bottom of the opposite page, Faneesh had drawn the shadow of a little girl with disheveled hair, reaching out with her long arms to hold the sun at the top of the page as many books, open and closed, fluttered around her. The drawing seemed naïve and funny, but I felt deep down that it was saying something profound. I turned the page and didn't deny to myself that I was starting to feel some enjoyment in reading her journal:

06/25/2005

Today, my father sat down and looked like he was about to cry. I was about to turn eighteen, on a night with no electricity and no moonlight. There was just the light of a candle that resisted being extinguished. He told me in a few words that he needed my help. At first, I didn't understand what kind of help he wanted from me, but when my mother broke down and started sobbing, I understood. This story had been repeating itself in the neighboring houses—a father choked up by words, a mother crying bitterly, and a daughter heading for an unknown fate by going to the Gulf for work."

I remembered that Faneesh had told Amer some of these details on the way from the office in al-Ain to Muscat. I now recalled her confidence as she talked to Amer, and I remembered Amer's desire to hear more. Oh my. Was it possible that she had sat down with Amer later and told him the rest of the story without me? Maybe they had stopped talking at the pizza restaurant to avoid my anger. My heart sank even more when I remembered that if I had not seen Amer lending Faneesh some books, he may not have told me about it, and the damn devil may not have mentioned anything about the books had I not put her on the spot with my questions. I trust Amer. He was empathetic towards her, and he was always rooting for this marginalized group of people, as he would say. He deals with maids with the spirit of a novelist, not with the body of a vile man. But their understanding is limited, which makes them expect more.

I repressed my anger as I looked at her drawing on the next page. Upturned faces with open mouths. Many of the faces were welling up with tears. This time she had drawn them with a pencil.

Intrigued, I turned the notebook upside-down to be able to see the faces in an upright position. On the following page:

06/26/2005

I kept my silence the first day, and I didn't give my father an answer. Today, my father reopened the subject. My heart stopped, and the book fell from my hands.

"It's need, Faneesh," my father said in a trembling voice. "It's need that's pushing me to ask this of you."

Faneesh had left several pages empty. Maybe she was thinking of filling them later.

09/01/2006

Today, the new academic year at the university started. I am crying nonstop in my room. My father heard back from the trafficking gang that has arranged for my quick departure to Saudi Arabia. There, I came to know another side of life that did not include my mother's smiling face or my tender father or the wide, hungry mouths of my siblings. The promise that the gang had given my father about taking care of me until I arrived safely was not real. They slapped me repeatedly when I refused to let one of the gang members touch me, and I was harassed more than once. I swallowed my voice for fear of harsh beatings and punches that almost made me lose consciousness, all in the hope of obtaining my passport and entry visa to Saudi Arabia. I hoped to start a different life from that of my grandmother whose husband kidnapped her when she was nine years old, and then raped and married her. It was all part of the prevailing culture in Ethiopia, as my grandmother would say, but she refused to allow that to happen to her daughter, so she married her off to my kind father. Oh my. It was as if I was repeating my grandmother's story, but in a different way. The unjust agreement with the gang dictated that they would take half of my salary during my first year of service, in return for the passport and visa to Saudi Arabia. And every delay in payment meant an increase in interest.

I was surprised by her fluid narrative. I figured she must first be writing on regular paper and then copying her writing into the journal in nice handwriting. She had tucked some sheets of paper that looked like drafts, with words crossed out and some revisions, into the middle of the notebook. It seemed that this notebook was very important to her, as she had taped some leaves, dried flowers, and ostrich feathers to the next page.

09/09/2005

Today my new life began. I arrived at the house of the first family that I would work for. The family had a Filipina maid who took care of the children, mopped, and cleaned. The lady of the house told me, verbatim, "I wanted to get a second maid for the dirty work." And, truly, here I was cleaning the bathrooms, kitchen, and closets, taking out the trash, tending the garden, and pruning the trees. I worked so hard, in a way that far exceeded the lazy work of the Filipina maid Vickie who made three times my salary.

All she did was sweet talk the three children, change their clothes, and feed them. The lady of the house complained about her laziness and about her not doing the cleaning like she should, but Vickie used the children as an excuse. In an effort to gain the approval of the lady of the house, I quickly learned the different types of detergents and the manner of cleaning that would satisfy her. Vickie conspired with me because teaching me how to clean spared her the burden of getting into verbal fights with the lady. Very quickly, I learned how to clean the expensive things, make the windows and floors sparkle, and freshen up the air. I even started watching Vickie as she put on gloves, chopped up and cooked vegetables, boiled delicious chicken, used paper towels to absorb all the oil, and made salads. The common language between us was very funny—some English sentences sprinkled with Arabic words that I had picked up from the children's chatter or the broken Arabic that I learned from Vickie.

Vickie treats me with a strange sense of superiority. She reminds me every day to wash my hands, clip my nails, and cover my hair properly. I wasn't embarrassed by any of this for I was now discovering a new life that I knew nothing about. Vickie would tell me that she made much more than I did, received favors, and earned the trust of the lady of the house because in the Gulf, there was a consensus that a Filipina is always clean and educated and knows how to run things in a way that pleases the hearts of ladies. But she also told me that she was getting sick and tired of the three annoying children who always chased her around and that she was hoping that one day she'd have a life of her own.

At first, I was clumsy. Things would fall from my hands and break, and when I broke an expensive vase, the lady of the house said that it was many times more expensive than my salary, and she decided to withhold my pay. I kissed her hands and begged her to forgive my slipup, but she refused. I was scared that the gang would punish my family if they didn't get half of my salary, according to our agreement. And despite my attempts to please the lady, and despite my serious efforts to learn from Vickie, the lady got fed up with me after I dropped an incense burner on the rug of the living room, and the coals left an irredeemable hole in the body of the expensive rug. When I refused to return to Ethiopia, the lady decided to transfer me to another sponsor, and she sent me to her mother-in-law, Hajjah Moudi, and I had a whole new story with her.

Empathy seized my heart. I sensed her weakness and vulnerability. She had revealed to me the secret behind her seasoned training. My curiosity about her story with Hajjah Moudi gnawed at me. She had mentioned her name in our fleeting conversations, but I had ignored getting into it to avoid any involvement with her. I figured that she wasn't writing her diaries daily and that she would select from her drafts the excerpts that she wanted to transfer into her notebook. I figured that out because the dates were far apart from one another.

The commotion outside woke up the thief inside me. Where could I hide the notebook when she was going through every nook and cranny of my room every day? No place seemed safer for the notebook than the gold safe that stood in my closet, with its short stature, so I opened it quickly and told the two hugging bears, "you'll be just fine in here."

I went down quickly, like someone wiping off the trace of her crime, to the kitchen, where Faneesh was putting away the groceries that she'd just come back with. I glanced at her and then went into the study to check my email and print out the new chapter from Amer's novel. Here I was, being suddenly entangled with a novel that he had been writing all his life and with Faneesh's memoirs. I grabbed the twenty-five pages that I pulled out of the womb of the printer and put them in a translucent folder. I went back to the kitchen and said to Faneesh, "I feel like having some fruit and halloum cheese with Lebanese bread and a green salad." I sat in the living room and started flipping through the channels as usual, accompanied by my light dinner. Faneesh gave me the change with the receipt. She said that she bought a perfume that she liked and that was on sale for two and a half riyals and that it was the first time she'd ever bought something for herself with her salary. She seemed happy as she talked about how the supermarket was bigger than she expected and had so many things that she hadn't seen before. On previous trips, Faneesh had only seen the things that I did, and now that she'd gone by herself, she saw things that she hadn't noticed when I was there with her.

I went up to my room with Amer's novel. When I lay down on the bed, sleep assailed me, and I slept for over an hour. I woke up to the sound of knocking at the door. It took me a few minutes to realize that the knocking was real and that I wasn't dreaming. I threw a robe over my nightgown and looked at the alarm clock on the nightstand. It pointed to twelve-thirty. I approached the door and said in a voice that was not awake yet, "who is it?"

"Open the door, Madame, please. It's me, Faneesh."

Faneesh stood in front of me. She was wearing a nightgown that reached the middle of her legs, and her braided hair was disheveled. For the first time, I saw her without a headscarf. She looked different, and she resembled the girl with the funny, disheveled hair on the pages of the journal. Her body was shaking. She was holding a pillow in one hand and a blanket in the other. She staggered into my room before I gave her permission to come in. She looked like she was about to cry. I was getting ready to tell her, "Not again, Faneesh. You will not drag me into your rugged territory. This is where I'll put an end to this saga." But she beat me to it and started talking.

"Madame," she said. "The suicidal woman stole my journal."

She said that and started crying hard. I became weak again. Maybe because it was I who had stolen the journal.

"Why would she do that?"

"The woman who's capable of jumping from my head to yours can do anything."

"Is your notebook that important that she would want to steal it?" I asked. "Why would it be of any benefit to her?"

"Why would be it be of any benefit to her to enter our dreams?" she asked. "I'm shaking in my room, so far away, for fear that I might see her again. Please, Madame, let me sleep in your room."

Before she finished that sentence of hers, she put her blanket over my rug, rested her head, with its disheveled hair, over her pillow, and slept. I didn't say a word. I got dizzy in a spiral of exhaustion, and my heart beat fast, fearing that one of us might commit suicide. I found myself covering myself with my blanket and falling asleep.

The next day, I woke up to Faneesh's voice as she said, "Madame, it's one o'clock in the afternoon." Was it possible that I had slept for half a day without any running or panting, without any slobber or tears? I was filled with happiness, and I stayed put, enjoying the warmth of the blanket as the cold air from the air conditioner struck my face. I felt the muscles of my neck and shoulders as I wondered about what had kept her away from me last night.

I took a hot bath. I slathered my body with soap and my hair with shampoo. I wondered if the woman had retreated from my dreams because I had painted her running in the direction of the balcony. I put on a white cotton shirt and baggy jeans. I was disgusted by the rug that Faneesh had slept on. Could she have left lice on my rug? The thought terrified me. I put on gloves and folded the rug with the tips of my fingers and parked it close to the balcony so it would find its way to the laundry. I tossed the gloves in the trashcan then went to my mural. I climbed on the ladder and started adding details here and there. I painted her black dress, and I added some visual effects to convey speed around her protruding body.

I turned around to Faneesh who fired off a question.

"Madame, is she going to return my journal?"

"Maybe, yes."

"When?"

"When she's done reading it," I said. "Is there something in there that you're worried about?"

"I miss it."

"I'll buy you a new journal so you can write," I said. "What's important is that you go back to sleeping in your room."

"Thank you, Madame. Should I prepare some food for you?"

"I'll prepare it myself."

"Did she visit you yesterday?"

"Why do you ask?"

"Because your face is glowing, like she's left you alone."

I didn't answer her question. I went down to the kitchen. We cooked chicken stew and white rice. Faneesh wrote down the recipe for the dish and we talked—which wasn't usual—about spices. I don't like too much spice in my food. She told me about the hot sauces that she makes with peppers. I told her that sounded similar to Indian spices. We had food again on the kitchen table as we continued our conversation about women and color. She told me that women in Ethiopia celebrate warm colors and uniquely shaped accessories. She showed me some pictures on her phone of relatives of hers who embraced bright colors.

I went back to my room. I locked the door. I was torn between reading Amer's chapter and Faneesh's diary. I felt myself gravitating more toward the latter. Maybe because I had promised myself to return her journal to her, after the "spell" she'd cast on me was undone through reading. I was excited to learn about Hajjah Moudi's story.

04/23/2006

Today, I moved into Hajjah Moudi's house. She seemed easygoing and loving. She was not like her daughter-in-law, with her frowning face. I discovered after a brief phone call with my father that I needed every single Halala for the sake of the mouths that awaited me in Addis Ababa and for the sake of the gang that had doubled its demands because of the delay in payment.

I will work silently and calmly so I don't break things that are expensive or dear to the Madame's heart. I will try to understand her mood so I don't fall into the trap of a reduction in salary. I will wash my hands well before doing anything, and I will cover my hair in order to delight Hajjah Moudi's Muslim heart.

06/03/2006

I woke up today with an overwhelming yearning for my mother, father, and siblings. I prepared coffee. The smell filled the entire kitchen. I drank it black and cried by the back door of the kitchen. Hajjah Moudi, who has been abandoned by her children, showers me with more gifts and donations than I deserve. She talks to me about the Quran and about the prophet Mohammad and about the customs of Muslims.

She surprised me when she started repeating, "You have Muslim manners." Maybe because I don't go out, talk to the driver like her Indian maid Miri does, or chat up the guests. And the quality of my work measures up to that of maids whose race is superior to mine, as far as the comparison between us often goes.

09/24/2006

Today is the first day of Ramadan. Hajjah Moudi brought me along to one of her Zikr, remembrance of God, ceremonies. She said that she needed my help because of her old age.

Hajjah Moudi talked about Islam with tremendous love, and whenever she'd mention the Prophet Mohammed's name, her eyes would well up with tears. I have been accompanying her almost daily. Hajjah Moudi tasked Miri with doing the housework and freed me up so I could tag along with her. I would get my salary at the end of the month without knowing exactly what my job was. She is teaching me some Quranic ayahs—she explains their meanings and tells me stories, most of which I don't understand.

09/28/2006

I will never forget the look of vindictiveness that Miri directed at me when she saw me supporting the frail Hajjah Moudi with one hand and carrying the bag of gifts in another. It wasn't my fault that I'd become Hajjah's spoiled close friend!

10/17/2006

Today I wrote a letter to my father telling him how happy I was with the new lady. My father had written me about the few remaining months, after which we would be free from the burden of the gang's demands. He told me he was now able to secure the school supplies for my five siblings and that he was able to buy medicine for my mother, who started having severe infections in her stomach.

1/22/2007

Hajjah took me by surprise today when she asked me to take the photographs of her children off the walls of the living room and her bedroom. She was in a difficult mood, as she repeated, "Astaghfir Allah, I seek God's forgiveness." I gathered up the courage to ask her why, so she told me that the sheikh had said, "It is not permissible to hang pictures of people or put up statues. We don't have the ability to give them souls during Doomsday." I understood since I first set foot in her house that sheikhs are akin to prophets. They only tell the truth and nothing but the truth.

Hajjah Moudi doesn't do anything, big or small, without consulting the sheikh. The sheikh is many steps above the priest of our village. I remember when she told me, "Hand me my phone," as I was putting henna on her heels to help treat the cracks. She called the sheikh and asked him if the henna would invalidate her prayers. And I was surprised when she asked him if it was permissible for her to continue watching her favorite show, al-Shugairi's Khawatir. I used to watch the show with her, but I didn't understand much of it. She asked the sheikh if we shouldn't watch it since it included a few musical scores.

Her life doesn't go on without contacting the sheikh on a weekly basis. She asks the sheikh about her clothes, food, and going out and talking with relatives. She's committed herself to doing the most righteous thing, constantly asking herself, "Is this better than that? Or is that more appropriate than this?"

03/04/2007

I write this as I cry hard. My Ethiopian friends who work for other families and whom I meet during special occasions are repulsed by me. Some of them have threatened to tell my father about my suspicious visits to the houses where Zikr ceremonies take place and about me entering the mosque. I emphasized to them that I was helping the old Hajjah, who cannot go by herself because of her frail body, but doubt kept on plundering their hearts, which felt protective over Christianity.

05/20/2007

Today, Hajjah Moudi told me again, "You have Muslim manners." I went into the kitchen. She asked about her favorite coffee cup set. My heart pounding, I told her that one of the cups had broken the other day. I was picking up the tray from the living room when it slipped from my hands. She surprised me by saying that she didn't care about the cup and that all she cared about was my honesty. She gave me a bottle of perfume as a reward. She said some kind, tender words to me. Her words delighted me, as much as they made me apprehensive of her. I lit a candle in my room and prayed to the Virgin Mary, asking her not to abandon me.

09/13/2007

I cried over my father's letter until the letters merged with one another and the words became smudged. My mother's disease was getting worse. My father's wages from the coffee fields were shrinking because he was spending time with her. His financial commitments for my siblings were growing every day, as Hajjah Moudi chased me in pursuit of divine reward.

I flipped through three pages on which she'd pasted clippings from Arabic books. They referenced the Muslim migration to al-Habasha, away from persecution by Mecca's polytheists, which led to al-Habasha's Christians earning great stature in the heart of Muslims. She underlined the word "al-Habasha" and drew an arrow from it pointing to the word "Ethiopia," which she had written by hand in English. She marked up many sections from the story of Sayf Ibn Dhi Yazan, which was written during the Mamluk period and which revolved around the Arab-Habashi war. Faneesh had drawn more than once the shadow of the girl with the disheveled hair, as she laid her hand on her cheek or extended her arms, unable to reach the sun.

12/02/2007

Hajjah Moudi hired someone to teach me Arabic so I could read the Quran. I also learned how to read and write a little bit of Arabic. I memorized some of the short prayers and learned Ayat al-Kursi, the Throne Verse, by heart without really understanding any of it. I study the Quran and Arabic during the day and cry in the arms of the Virgin Mary at night. I feel delirious and can't find a way out of my predicament. Hajjah Moudi is waiting for me to say something. She is making many insinuations. She waits and waits. She asks me if faith has taken a hold of me, and all I say is "Inshallah, God willing."

On the opposite page, Faneesh had glued a picture of an old church. She gave the girl a frown, and this time the girl's disheveled hair fell flat against the sides of her face. I felt the face's deep sorrow. I turned the page excited to find out what happened between her and Hajjah Moudi.

10/03/2008

Hajjah Moudi told me, "It's not good to read the Quran and enter God's places of remembrance with this name of yours. What about a name like Amira or Hasina or Sarah? I think the name Sarah is easy on the tongue and would be suitable. I nodded, approving my new name. I didn't have any other choice. I shook, fearing that one of the Ethiopian maids who knew my family in Addis Ababa would snitch on me. Hajjah Moudi cornered me with questions about what I wanted to be, and whether I thought of myself as a Christian or a Muslim. I felt dizzy and overwhelmed, as fear of my father, my siblings, my entire family, and even God gnawed at me.

11/05/2009

I donned the flowy hijab of Muslim women. It was different from my hijab, which used to consist of a scarf wrapped around my curly hair. I wore a long, black robe. I put a niqab over my face and went to the mosque. Women came from all corners of the world, and the black abayas swelled around me like black clouds on a rainy night. The sheikh arrived with a luminous face, his long beard mixed with white. A brown spot that had almost turned black appeared in the middle of his forehead. His body looked like a sack of rice, his potbelly sticking out in front of him. He stood in front of me sternly. I didn't know if I should look him in the face or plant my eyes on the ground. He asked me to repeat the two shahadas after him. My heart was ripped from its place. I couldn't find it in my ribs or in my hands or by my feet. I don't know where my heart had fled. I sweated profusely.

My father had raised us with a strict upbringing, and he wouldn't allow us to cross the line when it came to being disciplined before God. Every time our finances took a hit or our situation worsened, he would take us to church to pray. Oftentimes, God would alleviate our distress, and oftentimes I felt God's closeness to me. I remembered the church, the ringing of bells, my calm steps as I walked to church, and my hand in my father's hand. I remembered the Eucharist that I'd had when I was young. The face of the Virgin Mary appeared before me, and then she turned her sad face away from me. I almost hugged her as I repeated after the Sheikh, "Ash-hadu alla ilaha ill Allah, wa ash-hadu anna Muhammadan Rasulullah. There is no god but God and Muhammad is the messenger of God," without awareness on my part, as if another woman had occupied my voice and being. It wasn't me who had said that. It wasn't me.

I spent the night I converted to Islam thinking about God and if he was any different from how he used to be before. Would his compassion change now? Would fortune smile upon me, or would the Virgin reject me and be angry with me forever? The questions gnawed at my young brain. I lit a candle and asked her to forgive me.

The girl with the disheveled hair has her back turned to us on the following page. I know very well that maids lie a lot, that they fabricate stories to earn our affection. But Faneesh didn't write her life story to gain my compassion. At that moment, I wished that the disheveled girl would turn her face so I could see her. But she didn't. Despairing, I turned the page.

11/06/2009

Hajjah Moudi threw a party at her house and invited women without worrying about the number of guests. Money and gifts fell on me like rain. An old lady was so happy with me that she took off her gold necklace and put it around my neck. A woman hugged me and cried hysterically as if she'd seen the paradise that God has promised his believers. All the women leapt to their feet in order to hug me. I couldn't breathe at that moment, and as soon as they let go of me, I broke down and cried nonstop. One of the women said, "Look at the happy tears in Sarah's eyes, the woman who has converted to Islam."

Faneesh left a few colorful, perfumed pages empty, saturated with whiteness. I wondered what Faneesh could have written in that space. I wanted to learn more about her anguish, about all the fear and torment she suffered. I found myself following her story eagerly.

01/01/2010

Mrs. Moudi's single occupation has become asking me about my prayers. "Did you perform your morning prayers? Your noon prayers? Are you reading the Quran? Are you reading the book in English about the prophets' stories that I gave you as a gift? Sarah, here are some tapes that you should listen to. It's by a prominent advocate. Sarah, you should follow this channel on TV. It will put you on the straight path."

I no longer recognize myself since becoming Sarah. I needed over a year to forget my name "Faneesh" and remember my new name. The more I forget my old name, the more I forget myself, my customs, and my other life. Mrs. Moudi would say, "It's as if you've been born again."

09/02/2010

As I melt in my crying fits, Hajjah Moudi gets excited, thinking that I'm in a state of reverence and that faith has taken a hold of me. I perform the five Islamic prayers that Hajjah Moudi has taught me without feeling anything, and at night, like someone who's making up for her sins, I make the sign of the cross on my chest and I pray with the reverence of those asking for forgiveness. I perform the fasts of Muslims and of Christians.

12/11/2010

Hajjah Moudi's brother, Dari, visited us today. That drunk, who was constantly peeping at the maids in the house, didn't get any positive attention from me, so he became more vicious and fiercer. I complained to Mrs. Moudi about him chasing me in the kitchen and in the yard, but she'd say one thing, "He's the guardian of this house. It's a shame for you to say anything about him that's not nice."

No one asks about Hajjah Moudi, not her children or brothers or sisters. The drunkard Dari is the one who visits her the most and sweet-talks her—his only goal is to get some money for drinking. Hajjah Moudi appreciates him so much, loves him, and delights in his visits. She treats him like a spoiled child and overlooks his shenanigans and the way he talks and his disgusting smell. It's as if she doesn't see or hear or smell him. His chasing disgusts me. If Hajjah Moudi sees anything she doesn't like, she yells angrily, "Put on some baggy clothes, and don't enter the majlis room in my brother's presence." I cover myself and avoid him, which makes him stick to me even more.

04/03/2011

Dari forced the door open with his shoulder and entered my room after Hajjah Moudi forbade anyone from having the keys to the maids' rooms. He came in, aroused. He attacked me. I kept on resisting and yelling. My yelling grew louder. He bit my thigh with his teeth like a wild animal, and I had no choice but to break a vase over his head. He fell down, passed out. The neighbors called an ambulance. They took me to the hospital, and then to the police station. The story got bigger and more complicated than I expected.

06/23/2011

I will never forget the last look that Hajjah Moudi gave me when she said, "There's no place for you in my home." I wanted to explain things to her, but she said. "If you hadn't done something to the man, he wouldn't have dared come close to you. It's too bad that Islam couldn't take over your heart."

08/19/2011

Hajjah Moudi handed me the money and a ticket, without looking at my face. Going back to Ethiopia at that time, when my mother was starting to get treatment at the hospital, would have meant slow death for her and my father and my siblings. I contacted one of the gang members and asked him to find me work anywhere in return for some money.

I don't know if something had gotten in my eye at that moment or if a real tear was about to abandon my eye and attack my cheek. What I know for sure is that my heart shook between my ribs. I was irritated at myself for reasons that I didn't know at that moment. But my irritation kept growing at the same pace, constricting my breathing.

04/05/2012

I obtained an entry visa to Dubai. I didn't stay there for long. I got a job working for a kind family of Lebanese origin. But the family soon decided to travel abroad because the husband got a scholarship to study in England. I begged the lady to transfer the sponsorship to one of the offices and not send me back to Ethiopia, so she transferred the sponsorship to one of the employment agencies in al-Ain.

HUDA HAMED

09/17/2013

I found myself today in a strange place, crowded with women of countless colors and shapes. I stayed by my small bag, which I slept on at night and sat on during the day. The owner of the place came in and started brutally kicking one of the women on her belly and legs. I understood from the others that she had let her boyfriend into her employers' house. So she was returned to the agency.

Many men and women entered and left. They looked at us as if they were looking at merchandise. My new friends rushed to talk about their unique traits: what they know, their years of experience, and their salaries. I remained seated on top of my bag, waiting for someone to kidnap me into another life.

What a strange story. How many good stories did this woman possess—stories that would be good for a film or a TV series? Who was she now? A Muslim or a Christian? How did she think? Questions whirled in my head as I returned the journal to the closet.

FIF15EN

A LONG TIME had passed before I even thought about leaving my house. I put on an abaya, to which I had added a piece of velvet in dark red around the chest area and down the edges of the sleeves. I wrapped my head with a sheilah, allowing a few highlighted golden locks to drop down the sides of my face. I went by al-Fikr bookstore in al-Khuwair and bought a new journal that had a heart-shaped lock and a key that looked like the ones you see in cartoons. The notebook was green, with violet roses on its cover. Its pages were colorful and scented. Then I bought myself some new paint from the Shah Nagardas Stores in al-Qurum before heading to the City Center Mall to buy some underwear for Faneesh. I estimated that she was two sizes smaller than me.

I returned home and called Faneesh in a happy tone of voice, like someone atoning for her sins. She came out the guest bedroom running, a cleaning rag in her hand. I handed her the journal and the bag with the underwear. She took them from me and thanked me. I thought she was going to be ecstatic, so her cold response hit me like a slap in the face.

"Faneesh," I said. "You can go back to writing your diaries again."

"Thank you, Madame," she said. "I don't think I'll do that."

"Why not?"

"Why would I write?" she said. "So she can steal my thoughts and stories like she'd stolen my dreams before?"

Faneesh withdrew, disappointed and sad. The thief's conscience woke up—annoying and belligerent—so I went up to the second floor and started contemplating the running woman with her head cut off, who ran like she was about to crush anything that stood in her way. I went into my room. I remembered Amer and the new chapter that he was waiting for my opinion on.

I liked her notebook. I liked the two bears that felt reassured in my hands. I sat back in Amer's rocking chair. I turned to the page that I had marked and started enjoying stories and entering magical worlds that I had not known before. Faneesh wrote about our big, clean house that was empty, except for books and paintings, about the small area that she saw of Muscat whenever she took out the trash, about the small number of guests who occasionally entered our home, about her secluded room and the noises that worried her at night, and about the visits of the suicidal woman and the horrors of waking up drenched in sweat and tears. She narrated the dream twenty-eight times, with minor deviations, and she wrote elaborately about the food she ate alone.

02/03/2013

I eat my meals alone at the kitchen table. Vickie no longer eats with me or speaks about the superiority of the Asian race. The Indian Miri no longer joins us in order to ask me with curiosity about what Hajjah Moudi had gifted me.

She wrote about Amer, about his kindness and extreme compassion, about the books he lent her, and about their conversation on the entire way back from al-Ain to Muscat. She wrote other stories that I was not aware of.

02/13/2013

Early this morning, Mr. Amer was on his way out to work as I was watering the trees with the hose. He stepped out of the car and took the hose from my hand. He said, "These trees should not be sprayed like that. They need to be inundated with water. As you can see, we're in a hot country." Then he smiled at me, and I was happy. It's rare for anyone to smile at me like that.

02/28/2013

My toothache had become intolerable. I opened up to Mr. Amer about it, so he took me to al-Harub Medical Center on al-Qurum Street, which he usually goes to. I had two choices, either to get the tooth pulled out or get a root canal. I was very scared of the second option. Mr. Amer sat across from me and told me briefly that a little bit of pain meant that I get to keep my tooth. I agreed, just because of how excited he was about it. He took me to al-Harub Medical Center four times, for four consecutive weeks. He would buy me a sandwich and juice before each treatment, so I wouldn't get hungry. He'd ask me if I wanted a chicken or beef sandwich, if I wanted my juice with or without ice, and if the air conditioning in the car was reaching me or not.

I am not used to giving my opinion about anything. I accept donations, big or small. Mr. Amer encourages me to speak, and when I'm with him, I remember I am a woman.

03/05/2013

I liked my toothache. Being under the influence of anesthesia. The drilling tools that the doctor inserted in my mouth. I liked my voice when I talked to Mr. Amer. I don't know where my happy energy is coming from. My heart beats quickly, and life around me tastes differently.

HUDA HAMED

03/15/2013

I feel intoxicated by the smell of Mr. Amer's cologne as I iron his clothes. I wish for his pile of clothes to never end, as if I'm on a date with him.

03/17/2013

My toothache has stopped. The talking between us has stopped. Oh, I'm so sad.

05/23/2013

The world spins around me the moment Mr. Amer enters the kitchen, his cologne beating him there. He asks me what I'm reading, and I tell him the name of the book and the chapter I'm on. His eyes sparkle with a happiness that makes my heart tremble and my words all jumbled.

05/29/2013

His dark color reminds me of all the things I love, my black continent and my coffee.

06/05/2013

Today is depressing. I put his suitcases in the trunk of his car. I heard him saying he's going to Africa. I cried when I was chopping the onions. I cried when I was washing the dishes. I cried even more when reading was no longer enjoyable at night.

06/17/2013

I have forgotten the sound of my voice in his absence.

I was not in there. I was not anywhere in the twenty-one pages she'd written since she'd first entered my home. Where was I? Did she not see me? I read everything she'd written, carefully, from the beginning. I read everything she'd written and crossed out in her drafts. She had not said anything about me. That lowlife, wretched woman. I threw the journal. It hit the door hard. The two bears ached, and the pages of her drafts got dispersed all over the room. I didn't care.

How dare she, this nasty woman, write everything about Amer, whom she saw only briefly, and fail to write about me, when I was there the whole time? My anger rose up, like a shot in my veins. I remained in my place, rocking back and forth, until I closed my eyes.

I found myself at the bottom of the stairs, alone. I don't know how I had gotten out of the rocking chair and gone down. The lighting was dim. I gulped when I noticed that the walls of my house were empty of paintings. My voice choked up in my chest, and I couldn't call Faneesh. I climbed the stairs quickly. I wanted to get to my room so I could close the door. A few more steps and I'd be there, but the flight of stairs seemed longer than usual. I got tired. I put my hands on my knees as soon as I reached the second floor. My room was now close. I grabbed the handle of the door to my room, which stood between the balcony and the mural. I felt the presence of someone in the dark hallway. My hands shook over the handle. From the corner of one eye, I saw the suicidal woman standing across from the woman I had drawn on the wall. Her black hair fell like a waterfall over her back.

The rocking chair shook under the impact of my sudden awakening. My heartbeats accelerated. I clung to what little air entered my lungs. I warded off the devil and read the verses of refuge three times. I looked right and left, fearing that she might come out of somewhere in the room. I feared her dropping down from the ceiling or emerging from under the tiles of the floor.

The yellow notebook, the two hugging bears, and the drafts were exactly as I'd left them. I picked up the papers, put them back in the notebook, and hid it again in the gold safe. I rushed out of the room. I watched the world from the balcony. The sun was about to set. I looked behind me. I turned on all the lights on the second floor. I went into Yusuf's and Raya's rooms and turned on the lights, as if I were expelling her with light. I ran again to my room. I took out the Yanni CD and stuffed the CD player with Surat al-Baqarah, "the Cow" chapter. I turned up the volume, and my heartbeat gradually went back to normal.

I went out to the mural. I stood in front of the woman with the cut-off head in the same way that the suicidal woman had stood. But did she know that I was painting her? Was she happy with my work, or was she angry?

I winced upon hearing Faneesh's voice behind me. She started asking questions, but I told her sharply, "it's none of your business," and before she left, I asked her to bring me the long kitchen ladder. I told her to grip the ladder tightly with both her hands and to keep her tongue trapped inside her throat.

The ceiling was high, and I'm scared of heights, but the voice of Sheikh Mishari al-Afasi reciting the al-Baqara made me feel safe as my body climbed the whole distance. I drew her head tilted on the ceiling. Her black hair swam in every direction. She looked like a woman drowning at the bottom of some sea or swimming in the air. Faneesh maintained her silence and her tight grip on the ladder so it wouldn't move from its place. I went down. I didn't say anything to her, and she didn't either. But my frowning face signaled to her to keep her mouth shut.

I asked her to clean the yard and the entrance of the house that faced the street. Faneesh grabbed the cleaning supplies and left, and I now had my opportunity. I went up to my room and got her journal and the spare key to her room. I went into her room and put the journal on the table where I had found it. The journal I had bought her was still in its place. I flipped through it quickly between my hands. She hadn't written anything in it. I left the two notebooks next to each other and left.

The thief's conscience inside me was now at peace. The obsessions calmed down. I made myself some tea with saffron. I called Raya and Yusuf who were drowning in final exams. They told me that they were coming back soon. I called Amer, and we talked about many things. I wandered off for a few moments to what Faneesh had written about him, and I was overtaken by wild thoughts. I tamed my thoughts until they calmed down. Amer wouldn't tire of talking about the smell of Zanzibar, its fields and restaurants, like someone talking about his new beloved. He asked me if I had read the new chapter from his novel. I pretended I was too busy painting the mural. I promised him to read it in the next few days. He promised me a speedy return.

SIX16EN

ANOTHER CUP of tea and another phone call with Ammi Hamdan, who had been immersed in his longing for Amer. I also returned a call that I had missed from Tarfa. She cursed me for not returning her calls and messages. I apologized to her, blaming imaginary commitments. She insisted that I go to Kazim al-Saher's concert at the Omani Opera House. She said she'd bought the tickets online. I hesitated a lot. Then Hind also insisted that I go to the concert with the two of them.

I wore an abaya from one of my designs. I had incorporated into it a piece of silk at the sleeves and in the cleavage area. The silk fabric was light green. The sheilah was draped loosely, halfway on my head, concealing some of my hair and exposing the rest. A third piece of the green fabric was incorporated into the center of the sheilah, topped by gemstones in the shape of little triangles that sat next to one another. I put on light makeup. I put dark kohl on my eyes, the way Amer liked. I put on some light-colored lipstick. I went down the stairs like a princess. I put on my high heels. I noticed that Faneesh was eyeing my unexpected departure. Her face loomed with questions that she didn't voice.

I went out into the world like someone leaving a prison that she'd chosen and loved. I met Hind and Tarfa near the main gate. I was stunned by the Opera building that I was visiting for the first time. It looked like something out of the *One Thousand and One Nights*. Inside the big hall, where Kazem al-Saher stood across from me, I was ecstatic at the sight of the beautiful balconies and engravings. I don't love Kazem al-Saher as much as my two girlfriends do. I had come out so that I could escape. I relaxed my body and rested my head on the back of the chair and thought of Amer. I missed him more than ever. The kohl on my eyes ran down my cheeks.

SEVE**17**TEEN

AMER WOULD BE arriving at eight in the evening. I was ecstatic. I felt like dancing along with the Lebanese singer Elissa as she sang, "all this happiness that I'm feeling, it's all thanks to you." I missed him. My heart trembled like it did during our first dinner in Egypt, like it did when Amer planted the wedding band on my ring finger on our wedding night, like it did with our first hug and kiss.

I shook the nightly visitor out of my mind, and I shook off Faneesh's memoirs. I opened up my memory, harkening back to the beautiful days. My married years had passed by so quickly, without being dampened by marital troubles. I was the cause of envy among girlfriends every time we got together for coffee. They had hundreds of stories to tell about negligent husbands who didn't remember their anniversaries or birthdays or didn't bring presents when they returned from their travels. I was the cause of their envy because I didn't have anything to say about Amer, for I had been spoiled since the first day I set foot in his house. It wasn't because Amer didn't have any personality, as my parents thought, or because I had him wrapped around my finger or because I cast a spell on him, as my girlfriends like to joke, but maybe because we gave each other space. We each have our own life. I'd dive into painting and designing abayas and sheilahs, and he'd dive into his office to read and write. We'd meet over cups of coffee and tea like friends do, and we'd talk about many things. Travel would separate us, and our longing would grow like a mischievous child. Amer would go around the world and spend days in the desert only to come back to my lap like a bird who can only rest in his own nest. We cherished our presents from each other and special occasions together. Something would grow between us that we didn't name or talk about much. Amer would open up his arms to absorb my anger, rage, crying, and complaining, and I'd leave his arms a luminous butterfly. I would become his friend and his lover and his mother.

Faneesh came into my room, almost running. She waved her yellow journal in front of my eyes.

"Madame," she said. "She's given it back to me."

"Didn't I tell you that?"

"She read it. I was sure she would."

"How do you know that?"

"Because I arrange the drafts in the order that I write them," she said. "She left them out of order."

She wanted to add something else, but I put an end to the situation by turning my back and leaving the room before ruining her happiness about the journal's return and my happiness about Amer's return.

I didn't know what to wear today. I straightened my short hair that had grown until it touched my shoulders. I turned my face between my palms more than once, looking for signs of aging. My face looked a little tired. I gently slapped my cheeks so that they would become flushed. I wrapped my hair so the heat from the cooking wouldn't mess it up. I prepared the harees soup with meat that Amer liked and a green salad. Dessert was going to be Um Ali, which I elevated by adding some Omani bread and nuts and another plate of Omani balaleet and a pot of Karak tea. Amer's taste in food is traditional. He's not adventurous when it comes to food. I asked Faneesh to take the small table from the sitting room up to my bedroom. I put on it the red tablecloth with bright pink hearts. Faneesh set the food and plates on the table. I arranged the spoons and forks inside the napkins, like they do in five-star restaurants, and I placed red candles at the center of the table. Faneesh put lit coals in the engraved brazier, to which I added the perfumed oud sticks that Jokha had given me as a gift and that I had saved for special occasions. The scent filled the air. I took a deep breath. Oh, my . . . Jokha and her magical concoctions!

Faneesh welled up with questions, but I smothered any attempts at conversation. I wanted her to stay at the red light. I wasn't going to tell her about the secret behind having food in the bedroom or about Amer's return. I was going to leave her hanging.

I put on a red silky short-sleeve shirt and a black skirt. I restyled my hair. I went down to the living room and kept flipping through the channels as I waited for him. I regretted not going to the airport to pick him up and leaving this task to his friend. I watched the time that deceived me with its slowness. I looked at my watch, at the wall clock and the clock on my phone, as if I suspected that one of them was lying.

I noticed the door open. Amer staggered inside with two suitcases. I ran toward him. He hugged me and kissed me on the cheek. We sat together in the living room, our questions and stories overlapping. We had so much to tell one other. Faneesh passed by, smiled at Amer, and greeted him. Amer smiled at her and asked how she was doing. When she was about to leave, Amer called out to her and said, "Faneesh, I have something for you."

I swallowed my anger as I saw him open the outside pocket of his suitcase and take out a medallion with dried cloves dangling from it.

"You should put it in your room so you can remember the smell of Africa," he said laughing.

Faneesh was delighted as she took it from his hand and thanked him, happy.

He had given her a present before me. Maybe because her present was in the outside pocket of his suitcase. Maybe he was saving my presents for a more private moment. For sure, he wasn't trying to get her attention or he wouldn't have given her the present in front of me. I asked him to go up to our room. Amer was surprised to find a dining table with lit candles close to the bed.

He said, "oh my, so much action! I'm starving!"

He washed his hands, and we sat next to each other. I scooped up some food for him. I fed him with my hands, and he did the same. My longing for him overwhelmed me. I showered him with kisses and hugs, and he enveloped me with so much affection that didn't subside until late that night. My mind wandered off during our intimate moments. Faneesh's face haunted me. I imagined her with her long ears glued to our bedroom door. I imagined her monitoring our feverish, longing breaths. I repressed my moans so she wouldn't hear us. My enjoyment of Amer's body waned a little, but he soon reignited my passion and desire, until Faneesh's face vanished.

We woke up like newlyweds— with lovesick laziness, whose delirium we enjoyed for hours. Then we went downstairs. We had breakfast, talked, laughed. Faneesh came in and out more than once. She took away dishes and brought others. I didn't see her, didn't pay any attention to her. I was too busy with Amer, too busy with the television, and with looking right and left. Amer asked me if I'd read the chapter he sent me, and I told him about all the things that had kept me busy. He told me he was going to work on finishing the novel soon since he now had good writing material. He was excited as he talked about it. We went up to the second floor again. Amer noticed the woman running toward him with her head hung at the ceiling. He stood there, stunned, for a few moments.

"Zahiyya, who is this giant woman?"

I didn't say anything. I didn't have a good answer. I didn't know where to start the story.

He added, "She's scary. Why did you paint her on Raya and Yusuf's wall?"

"So I can stop her from coming into our home."

We sat together calmly in the swing on the balcony, with our backs to the woman. I told him about the dream. How it started and how it evolved. I started talking about my dream but didn't say a word about Faneesh's dream. Amer was very moved. He held my hands gently and didn't say a word. He didn't believe in dreams, and he saw them as being outside the realm of logic. He had not believed the story of the woman who had visited me in a dream and given me the news about Raya and Yusuf. He never believed that she was the one who had given them their names.

Amer grabbed me by the hand and walked me into the room. He opened his suitcase. He took out my presents. A colorful African dress and beautiful gemstones and perfume, in addition to other decorative things for the house. I was delighted by the presents.

He added color to my life and brought me joy. Once again, we were entangled in each other's arms.

We went to visit Ammi Hamdan. Amer hugged his father warmly and greeted his mother Jokha, kissing her on the head. Jokha had prepared a lavish feast in celebration of Amer's return. Tharid meat stew, chicken kabuli, and irsiyya with tarsha sauce. Jokha loaded our plates with delicious food. She insisted that we eat more and more so she wouldn't get depressed about us not liking her food. She served Amer a plate and looked at him, awaiting a compliment or a sign of admiration. Amer swore that he had never eaten anything tastier than the food made by Jokha's hands. Jokha puffed up like a rooster. I shot him a look from the corner of my eye, which prompted Ammi Hamdan to burst out in infectious laughter.

Jokha sat down to eat her food slowly and didn't leave the room as she normally did. Her longing for Amer and her curiosity about the stories that Ammi Hamdan eagerly awaited, like a smitten lover, kept her at the table. But Ammi Hamdan dashed her hopes by not asking any questions about Bi Soura. I assumed that Amer had been in touch with him the whole time, telling him as he had told me all the big and little details. The subject that was the star of the evening was Saeed Bin Zaher al-Mahrouqi, the man whom Amer was advised to go see to inquire about his mother Bi Soura. Saeed al-Mahrouqi had not been to Oman since he'd left it at five years old except for one month, during which he felt like a fish out of water.

"Saeed al-Mahrouqi knows all the Omanis well," he said. "He knows all about their spouses and children. He moves around a lot because of his clove business. At sixty, he is tall, skinny, and dark with a sharp memory and tons of stories. His language is an odd combination of Omani dialect, English words and lots of Swahili expressions, some of which I was beginning to understand and others that I just guessed from context." Ammi Hamdan was delighted. "Those were the days," he said. "How did you find al-Mahrouqi?" Amer patted his father's leg, stretched out parallel to him. He said, "He was a bit reserved at the beginning. But as soon as he knew that I was Amer Bin Hamdan al-Rawahi, nicknamed 'the Swahili,' he hugged me warmly. I knew at that moment that he was your best friend."

Ammi Hamdan nodded his head like someone who'd become intoxicated by images that blossomed in his memory. "Son, Saeed lived on the Tanzanian mainland, and the clove business brought us close together," he said. Ammi Hamdan wrapped chunks of meat with a piece of Omani bread soaked with gravy and took one bite after the other. "Saeed's father, may God have mercy on his soul, used to wake up empty-handed, unable to provide anything for his wife and children. He was destitute. And now, mashallah, Praise God, he's one of the big names in the al-Dakhiliyah governorate. A long time ago, a person was considered lucky if he owned a few palm trees that could keep himself and his children from starving. We'd refer to him as 'the guardian of fortune.' Palm trees meant capital and life."

Stunned, I asked Ammi Hamdan, "So, those who didn't have any palm trees just starved to death?"

He said, "During famines, yes. Some people starved to death."

Ammi Hamdan relaxed into his cushion, licked the gravy off his fingers, and kept on talking. "Abu Saeed, Saeed's father, used to work in the fields as far as I remember. He'd harvest dates, water the plants from the canal, cut up and clean the fruit, dig wells, and take the fruit to the market. His wages consisted of a bag of dates or wheat grains or feed for his livestock, and the generous ones would hand him some tips. Umm Saeed, Saeed's mother, may God have mercy on her soul, used to work milling grain. She would grind her neighbor's wheat grains or coffee beans, bake bread for them over the tawbaj griddle, and sew their clothes. And the women would give her bread or coffee and hand-me-down clothes. That's how life went on. One day they might have had something, but the next day they may not have had anything at all."

Amer put a lot of the raisin-infused sauce over the irsiyya. He said, "I was very surprised that Saed al-Mahrouqi talked about Zanzibar as if it were God's heaven on earth, Paradise itself, and salvation from poverty and helplessness." Ammi Hamdan nodded his head in confirmation. "It used to be like that, Amer, but the situation is different now."

Jokha ate slowly, rarely raising her head up from the plate. She handed Ammi Hamdan a few dates. "Exactly as you said, Amer," Ammi Hamdan said. "Zanzibar was portrayed to us as the eternal salvation from poverty, hunger, and unemployment. I remember, Amer, when my father and I joined a caravan that left from Adam to Mahout. We left destitute, with nothing to protect us from starving. We gave the few piasters we had to the captain of the sailing ship. It depended on trade winds for its movement. The ship had parked far from the dock, so my father and I and the rest of the travelers went down to the small boat. Travelers from Oman used to travel through Muttrah or Seeb, but those of us leaving from the inner and eastern areas had to leave from Mahout." Amer interrupted him as he poured milk tea with ginger from the pot, "From Mahout to Zanzibar nonstop?" Ammi Hamdan laughed. "We almost starved to death. The journey, which was set up based on the trade winds, took eighteen days. But the winds weren't always on our side. We had to stop in Mirbat and Aden and Mogadishu." Amer rested his arm on the red and brown cushion in the Arab-style sitting area. "What about food?" he asked. Ammi Hamdan adjusted his posture. "The caravans stopped in Mambasa where we'd stock up on fresh water. As for food, it was usually dates and baby shark."

We finished eating dinner. Amer's sisters brought us coffee with jawwal al-asal, a honey-based dessert. Ammi Hamdan said, "Today, Jokha is celebrating her son Amer's return from his travels." Jokha patted Amer's shoulders happily. "Amer's return means the world to me, wallah." I hadn't noticed before that Jokha loved Amer the way mothers loved their eldest sons. I noticed tears in her eyes. I noticed how happy she was when he complimented the tasty food she had prepared. Amer pressed on Jokha's fingers affectionately. "Mother, jawwal al-asal can't be our dessert," Amer said. "It's very heavy to eat after dinner." Jokha insisted that he taste it. She tried to playfully coerce him, and he was acting out like a spoiled child. Then he succumbed to her desire and ate some.

Ammi Hamdan resumed, "Cloves made us friends. My father and I worked in the shamba, and Saeed and his father worked in exporting cloves through the big companies. Saeed loved learning and reading. We saw each other a few times a year. We exchanged books and a passion for politics."

Amer got up immediately and took presents for his mother Jokha, siblings, and Ammi Hamdan out of the extra suitcase. They were delighted. In addition to the wrapped present he gave her,

Amer handed Jokha all sorts of spices, and she almost sneezed when she brought them close to her nose to smell them. His younger brothers loved the wild tigers printed on the shirts he got them. His sisters loved the cotton kaftans and the colorful lesos. We were all eager to see Ammi Hamdan's gift. It was a small gift, wrapped carefully. As Ammi Hamdan opened it, we opened our eyes wide to see what it could possibly be. It was a CD of old songs whose value only Ammi Hamdan knew. Amer said, "The complete works of Fatima bint Barka Bi Kidude." Ammi Hamdan repressed a tear as he flipped the CD in his hands. He asked his daughter Shamsa to open it and play it on her device. The music filled the room. Everybody stopped talking, trying to figure out why these songs were such a big deal. Ammi Hamdan said, "I'm sure it was the rascal Saeed al-Mahrouqi who recommended you get this." Amer nodded his head in confirmation.

We didn't understand any of the words. I raised my voice over the music, "Ammi Hamdan, what do these lyrics mean?" He was quiet for a moment. "This song is usually sung to the bride on the night of her wedding. I don't really know how to translate it. OK, the song says,

If enjoying marital life is your goal
then you better keep your clothes on when eating with your husband
Bring him the spices so he can get dizzy
Give him some fancy tobacco."

I laughed until I almost choked. Ammi Hamdan explained, "Zahiyya, the lyrics are much deeper than what might seem on the surface. This woman sang in different countries around the world. She visited Muscat twice, and I never missed seeing her in concert. She's got something special, this woman." After keeping her silence, Jokha said, "The music sounds to me like it's Gulf Arabic." "They are playing the doumbek drums," Ammi Hamdan responded. "Fatima was born at seven months. 'Bi Kidude' means 'tiny one.' Her nickname stuck with her as she became famous. Oh, how I loved that woman, who was full of life and kindness and vivaciousness and sarcasm. Listen to this part. She's saying, '*when you take Uthman's goat to graze, make sure the grass is dewy.*'" Ammi Hamdan translated another section where she sang, "*When the goat is full, she returns home all by herself.*" Jokha and I burst out in laughter, together this time. We were like a deaf man at a wedding. We had no clue what was going on. Ammi Hamdan said in a serious tone, "You won't really know what's between these lines, the political message behind these words. It's saying that when the people are well fed, they will go back home on their own. They will live in peace under the government, without the need to use a stick."

Amer said, "Her fame goes all the way back to the days of Sayyid Khalifa bin Harub, Zanzibar's Omani Sultan. When she died, the Tanzanian president attended her funeral. She's a prominent singer."

I tried to enjoy the words like they did, but the language barrier prevented me from feeling the words. Ammi Hamdan and Amer were enthralled by her voice. They were busy talking about her and discussing the meaning of the lyrics, while Jokha and I exchanged looks and laughter.

I shifted the conversation to another topic and asked the question that had been haunting me since the beginning of our gathering, "How did Saeed al-Mahrouqi become a rich man?"

Ammi Hamdan said, "He had the same kind of support the rest of us did in the beginning. The Arab Association, and by that,

I mean the Omani Association, hosted everyone. It was headed by Abdullah Bin Suleiman al-Harithi, who served as its president for thirty years." Amer put his arm over the cushion behind my shoulders, so that I was now closer to him. He said, "Saeed al-Mahrouqi told me that the Arab Association built a mosque in every area, to which they added rooms for rent. Any traveler could stay there and get food for free. He could even get a small loan to help him start a small business." Ammi Hamdan nodded in agreement. "The Arab Association helped us get on our feet. It gave us money, money that helped some of us become rich."

Amer went back to tapping his hand behind me. He said, "Unfortunately, the association stopped working during the coup and was only resurrected later. By the way, Saeed mentioned that those who lived in the city like you and Grandpa, may God have mercy on his soul, had some stability. They lived under a highly civilized and progressive government and were more educated and sophisticated. He said that if it were not for the coup, they may have never gone back to Oman. But those who lived in mainland Tanzania like Ammi Saeed were traveling to Oman on a regular basis, and their relationship with Tanzania was a temporary one." Ammi Hamdan agreed. "That's true, Amer. Those who lived in the capital lived in luxury, and their children received scholarships to study in Baghdad, Cairo, and Damascus. Of course, I was an exception because my father had a different perspective regarding mixed schools that included Africans. Those Omanis who lived on the mainland were far from the influence of the central government and the impact of its services."

I said jokingly, "Ammi Hamdan, Amer is bringing up all these stories so he can write his novel." Ammi Hamdan's face lit up, "I have been waiting for this moment since he was in fifth grade. He would write and hide his papers away from my eyes, and sometimes he'd insist on reading me his writings."

Amer lifted his arm from behind me. "There are many things that I want to say and talk about, but Zanzibar is a story that does not end. You know, father, I noticed that an Omani looks for his tribal lineage even when traveling. Can you imagine that Saeed's father crossed all these distances only to settle into his tribal order again? As soon as he arrived, he asked the Arab Association about where the other Mahrouqis lived. Then he went with this son to the Tanzanian mainland near the Kajera River. There, Saeed found the paradise that his father promised him. The big river, the vast greenery, and the moderate weather all year around."

Ammi Hamdan turned the demitasse coffee cup between his index finger and thumb. "Those were the best times, Amer. The one image that I can't get out of my head is that of my dry, vicious, and angry father lined up among the other men during Eid festivities and waving his cane as he danced the Azwa sword dance. Those were among the rare times he ever smiled. The sound of the clanking of swords and the glistening daggers on their waists were legendary in that place, Amer," he said.

Amer grabbed a cup, stirred the pot, and poured a new cup of coffee for his father. "You had a good relationship with Saeed's father," he said. Ammi Hamdan shook the cup between his hands as he returned it, empty, to Amer. "For the longest time, I wished he were my father. Do you know where Saeed's open-minded father, who loved life and education, took us one day? You won't believe it. He took us to the house of Hashel Bin Rashed Bin al-Maskari, the editor of the al-Falaq newspaper. Saeed and I were big fans of his. Saeed's father was still very poor at the time al-Maskari invited us for lunch at his al-Madfaa house. He felt so grateful and so happy for his hospitality. He didn't know how to express his gratitude except by giving him a pen that he'd bought in Oman for five baisas." "Oh my God," Amer said as he smacked his thigh. "You never told me before that you met al-Maskari." Ammi Hamdan shook his head. He said, "It was the first and last time I saw him." As if his nostalgia had awoken from some place in the heart, Ammi Hamdan went back to asking questions. "Tell me," he said. "Did you go to the Corniche al-Fardani?" Amer said, "We walked there in the evening, me and Ammi Saeed. The smells of tasty grilled shrimp, meat, and chicken assaulted our noses the whole time we were there." Ammi Hamdan asked, "Did Saeed tell you why he returned to Oman even though their business was doing well?" Amer said enthusiastically, "Of course I asked him about that. He told me the story of the sip of water."

I found myself salivating over al-Mahrouqi's tales as if I was going to write his story. "What's the story about the sip of water?" I asked. Amer looked at me. "One day, Zahiyya, a group of Africans knocked on Saeed's door. When he opened the door, they said a lot of things to him, and ended their words with the sentence, 'the son of a snake is a snake,' Ammi Saeed laughed, thinking it was a compliment, like the expression, 'the son of a lion is a lion.' As soon as he went back inside and told his father what they had told him, his father's face tightened. Saeed's feelings about that saying changed. He finally understood what it meant when he was walking over the river bridge, as he was heading back from one of his sales tours and came upon some African soldiers humiliating

HUDA HAMED

his father. They asked him to put his hands over his head as his father kept on repeating one phrase in Omani dialect, 'I swear, I won't take a sip of its water.' He repeated the phrase over and over. Ammi Saeed screamed in the soldiers' faces, telling them in Swahili, 'my father needs water. Why won't you let him have some? He's thirsty.' I must clarify, Zahiyya, that Saeed's relationship with Arabic is weak. He only understands its surface meaning. When he went back home, he found his father packing up his belongings. He'd never seen him so angry before. His father told him that they were returning to Oman and ordered him to pack his things. When he asked, 'why are we going back?', his father started yelling in his face. 'Didn't you hear me saying, I will not take a sip of its water? I meant that I won't stay here for another moment. I will not drink except from my country's water.' That was the incident that made Saeed al-Mahrouqi return to Oman."

Ammi Hamdan said in a serious tone, "Amer, there's another story that might justify the way some Africans treated Saeed's father. In the early seventies, Saeed was playing with some Omani friends who lived near his house. He raised his index finger in the face of his 'enemy' friends, pretending to shoot them. His 'gunshots' were nothing more than a spray of drool. He repeated, 'I am gonna kill you, Abeid Karoume. I'm gonna kill you.' News of what Saeed had said during the children's game spread all over the neighborhood . . . a week after that incident had happened, news of the killing of Abeid Karoume was broadcast on the radio, so Saeed's father worried about him and locked him up in his room, forbidding him from playing outside. He feared that people would say that he and his family had knowledge of the conspiracy to kill Karoume." Amer interrupted his father, "So Saeed al-Mahrouqi predicted the death of Abeid Karoume in a silly game, but it was Hamoud Mohammed bin Hamoud al-Barwani who shot him. He showered him with a barrage of bullets. Those close to him said the number of bullets reached twenty-seven. Saeed chased the shadow of Karoume, killing him a thousand times, but al-Barwani shot him dead in front of his guards and ministers who were armed to the teeth, without anybody being able to stop him." Ammi Hamdan said in an angry, frustrated tone. "Al-Barwani avenged all of us. He avenged our ruined dreams. He avenged the souls of Omanis. He avenged their honor that was violated collectively." Then Ammi interjected, "Amer, do you know why it didn't occur to us that Karoume would do what he did to the Omanis?" We all stopped talking, but Amer didn't respond. Ammi Hamdan added, "Because we didn't expect that Abeid Karoume would bite the very hand that took him in and raised him. He was raised in the home of Mohammed Bin Saeed al-Kharusi, which is why many people denied that his name would even appear on the list of coup plotters."

"What you all suffered during the coup was more brutal," Amer said. Ammi Hamdan responded, "The statement that shocked me and made my heart bleed, Amer, was the one I heard from Mohammed al-Ghazali, in a taped recording, saying that twenty thousand Omanis were slaughtered in one day, and no one shed a tear over them. Men, women, and children were rounded up and shot. They were loaded up into trucks and buried collectively. Omani manuscripts and documents were burned. Stamps were made to commemorate the damn memory. My heart hurts as I remember these events that were crossed out of our minds."

My heart shivered. I was shocked by the barrage of information that Amer and Ammi Hamdan exchanged. I felt as if I was outside the world. I was ignorant about most of what they said. I was ignorant about those stories, people, and deaths. I felt ashamed of myself, and I had a strange thirst to learn more.

EIGH**18**EEN

AMER YANKED US out of the sadness of the moment with the sound of his laughter. "I just remembered something, father," he said. "You're going to die from laughter, wallah, by God." Ammi Hamdan patted his shoulder and said, "Tell, tell." I had never seen them like that, so crazy and vivacious.

"Gamal Abdel Nasser's visit to Tanzania. Do you remember it?" Ammi Hamdan's laughter reverberated throughout the house, and tears gushed out of his eyes. "Wallah, I'll never forget that story," he said. Jokha interrupted their laughter. "Tell us the story," she said. Ammi Hamdan looked around and said, "Ooh, that was a huge deal for us at the time, given everything that we'd heard about the man. Of course, Saeed and I weren't able to see him, but we heard all about him from the local station. That day, Saeed's father brought a big poster of Abdel Nasser, which was almost half a meter in length, and hung it on the wall of the room. Saeed lost his mind. He went crazy! When he saw me, he took out the one picture of himself that never left his pocket. It was as tall as his pinkie. He said, 'Look Hamdan, we're adults, but see how small our pictures come out. How about that photograph of Abdel Nasser, which now occupies one-fourth of our wall? Can you imagine what he must look like in reality? I think if this man were to set foot in the Kagera River, the river wouldn't even reach up to his knees because he's so huge." Amer laughed, and Ammi Hamdan laughed. Jokha laughed too, and I laughed along with them.

I found myself enthralled in their conversation by the time I had my third cup of milk tea. "So, how did you use to communicate with your families in Oman a long time ago?" I asked. "The distances were vast." Ammi Hamdan got excited. "If you can imagine, Saeed's father was adamant about making sure that his son knew everything about his uncles, aunts, and the names of their children," he said. "He would read the letters that arrived from Oman as if he were reading the holy books. He would reread and examine them and then save them in a chest. He told Saeed about his paternal aunt Mizna when she had a baby that they named Mohammad. He told him about his maternal uncle Ali when he had a baby girl he named Aisha. Letters would tell us everything, who was born, who died, and who was going to follow us to Zanzibar. My father also used to send my uncle Taleb some money so he could buy him a piece of land with palm trees and a well, and my uncle would send back a letter telling him that he started the process of building a house. It all happened through letters, and the delight of receiving them was just unbelievable. We respected letters and would hold them, hug them, kiss them, and save them among our most valuable belongings."

Ammi Hamdan's face tightened. "Imagine, my daughter Zahiyya, that my strong father who upheld the theory that men don't cry, cried uncontrollably when he received the news about the death of his sick mother through a telegraph," he said. "It was unbelievable. He cried for an entire day. He locked himself up in his room that day and didn't go to work, he who never skipped work during all the crises that he'd been through. And when the news spread, those who knew us came by to offer their condolences. I felt at that moment that my father was grieving his estrangement, for he didn't get to hold his mother or hug her before her final goodbye."

I entered the fray of sweet and bitter stories. "And how did you used to send money?" I asked. Amer patted my shoulders and said jokingly, "Am I the one writing the novel here, or is it you, Zahiyya?" I laughed, and everyone around us laughed too. Jokha and her daughters got up and started picking up the dishes and making their way into the kitchen. Jokha found numerous excuses to come in and out of the room. She brought tea, coffee, and nuts, and even purified the house with her own incense concoction, saturated with musk and amber. Ammi Hamdan captured my attention with his answer. "There wasn't a direct way to transfer money to Oman," he said. "The transfers first went to India and then from India onto Oman. Sheikh Saif bin Hilal al-Mahrouqi, a wise, trustworthy man, would receive them and write down every big and small detail. And then uncle Taleb, my father's agent and the man in charge of taking care of his transactions, would receive the money."

Amer grabbed a handful of peeled almonds and walnuts. "What I don't understand well, father, and worry about dealing with in the novel, is the relationship between Africans and Omanis," he said. "Did you form sincere friendships with them, or were you perceived as mere occupiers from their point of view?" Ammi Hamdan got animated. "OK, there isn't one answer to your question, Amer," he said. "There are different perspectives. Many Africans loved the Omanis who entered their homes, ate their food, studied their Swahili language, and pursued an education sitting next to them at school. Some even married and had children with them. Many

Africans cried for the Omanis during the coup, and some helped them escape to safe harbors. But there's also another scenario that contradicts this one."

Amer stopped talking, and then asked, "Like what?" Ammi Hamdan said, "Like what happened to me and to Saeed and Yaseen. Did Saeed not tell you that story?" Amer shook his head no. Ammi Hamdan said, "Saeed and I used to like this tropical fruit whose name now escapes me. It just grew everywhere and didn't need to be planted. It was very tasty. But we were too short and couldn't reach it. We had an African Muslim friend called Yaseen. He loved us, and we loved and played with him secretly since my father would not allow that. Yaseen was tall and had broad shoulders. He suggested carrying me on his shoulders so I could pick a piece of fruit. Yaseen bent down, and I climbed gently on top. I found myself surrounded by countless fruit, so I grabbed one and tossed it to Saeed. As I picked a second one, I was terrified by the sound of someone screaming in Swahili. Yaseen flinched under my feet, and his shaking made me fall to the ground. We knew it was Yaseen's father. He said angrily, 'How could you stoop your back to those who occupied and enslaved you?' We never saw the African Yaseen after that day." Amer said, "Ammi Saeed told me another story that happened after the coup. It was about his nephew who participated in one of the national celebrations and repeated along with them an anthem that had a sentence that said in Swahili, 'whenever you see an Arab, slaughter him.' The child's father was seated at the podium. That night, the boy received a strong slap on his shoulders. That's exactly what Saeed referred to as the manufacturing of hate."

I went back to asking Ammi Hamdan about his friend Saeed and why he did not move back to Oman even though life circumstances had changed and power dynamics were different. He said, "My daughter, many Omanis didn't return and ended up staying there. It was different for Saeed. He suffered the shock of his dream." "Shock of his dream?" I said, surprised. Amer said, "Ammi Saeed did come back to Oman for one month only. He had grown up listening to the old folks talk about Falaj al-Malih, al-Sharia, Tawi al-Saleel, Mubairiz, Harat al-Rabhba, and Harat al-Shabina, and other countless details pertaining to mainland Oman. They talked about things and places that his memory no longer retained after leaving Oman as a child. The old folks' stories visualized Oman for him as a promised land, a dream."

I asked again about the secret of his shock. Ammi Hamdan gathered his thoughts. "I remember the day he came back, a few years after we'd returned to Oman. It was on May 12, 1973, at noon. The plane had landed in Bayt al-Falaj Airport. When we met, he told me that he had passed out, that it was about fifty degrees Celsius. His first shock was the scathingly hot weather and his constant nausea on the one-lane road from Bayt al-Falaj airport to Adam town. He'd returned with his father since he now had a farm and a house and plenty of cash in his pocket. The road was empty, with no buildings or trees on either side, except for what had sprung up by chance. The heat made his body boil over like a kettle on a hot stove."

Amer continued, "The second shock, as he had told me, Zahiyya, were the houses that he found exactly as he had left them. They were made of mud and had no bathrooms. Folks lived in them with their cattle." Ammi Hamdan laughed. "There was no electricity. His sister Wadha would bring water from al-Falaj in a jug that she carried on top of her head," he explained. "Saeed was shocked to learn that they didn't have water-supply systems inside the houses." Amer continued, "Imagine that Saeed's father was the first person to build a big house with bathrooms. The Ministry of Education rented it and turned it into a school!" Ammi Hamdan nodded in agreement. "Still, that didn't conceal his disappointment about people relieving themselves out in the open or bathing in the creek, whereas in Zanzibar, water was available inside people's houses. Princess Salma, who had married a German man, wrote in her memoirs that Germany was beautiful but that they didn't have electricity as they did in Zanzibar. They also had phones since the days of Mr. Barghash."

Amer resumed talking. "You know, the line that Saeed said and that I will never forget and will use in my novel was, 'they took me to Oman, on the account that it was a long-awaited dream, but I realized right at that moment that I had left the dream behind me.'" Ammi Hamdan became obviously emotional. I was so eager to learn the rest of the story. "And what did Saeed al-Mahrouqi do after all this shock?" Amer answered, "A month after his shock, he went back to mainland Tanzania. He went back to wandering between the clove fields and the library shelves."

Jokha put plates of nuts and fruit in front of us, and she changed our dirty plates with swift alertness. Amer pointed to his full belly. She smiled. "Today, we're just going to sit and stay up together." Jokha took the coffee cup from Ammi Hamdan's hand to stop him from drinking more. "It's not good for your health," she said. Ammi

Hamdan succumbed to her wishes. He said, "Tell me about your novel, Amer." Amer was quiet for a little while, as I cut up some apples for him. "There's something that I don't really know how to say or even describe," Amer said. "But I feel it so deeply like a knife in my throat. It's something that I'm trying to work on as a theme in the novel. I felt it even more strongly as I was reading Amin Malouf's book on 'deadly identities.' I want to talk about those returnees from Africa to Oman, those who lived in Zanzibar for many years but who are of Omani origins, origins that are deeply rooted in tribal heritage. But they have lost their identity, for they are referred to as Zanzibaris in the Oman to which they returned, whereas in Tanzania they are called 'Manga,' or 'Wa-Manga.'"

Jokha joined us and sat down next to Ammi Hamdan. "What's the meaning of Manga?" Jokha asked. Amer said, "Mother, Manga is not usually used except in reference to a fundamentalist Arab. And it's an adjective that is always associated with Omanis. Princess Salma referred to that in her memoirs too." Ammi Hamdan said, "There are tragicomic stories about that. A woman who was born in Rustaq and was from a well-known tribe had gone to Zanzibar with her husband, before passports existed, and stayed there for many years. When she wanted to visit Oman, she was asked to apply for a visa. She completely refused to do that. How was she supposed to enter her own country on a visa? After much insistence from her Omani family, who missed her and longed to see her, she decided to go to Dubai, and her family met her there so they could say hello. And there are other stories that are even funnier and more tragic. I remember a man who came to Zanzibar for a funeral. Then the coup happened, so the poor man was stuck in Tanzania for sixty years for a funeral visit that never ended." I said, "Oh my God, Ammi Hamdan, is it possible that these stories are real?" Waving his hand, he said, "Zahiyya, there are stories that have gone with the wind."

Amer said, "You know what, father? When I was walking with Saeed, an elderly man followed us after he noticed our distinctive white dishdashas. He too was wearing a white dishdasha and a turban. His veined hand shook over the cane. He surprised me by saying, 'come on over, come on over for some coffee.' His accent sounded like it had emerged out of al-Batina or Nizwa or Samail, or some other place I knew very well. It was the way he had said the word 'come on' with its original flavor, full of enthusiastic hospitality. We parted ways with the man after we greeted him, heard his news and told him our news, as is the convention. We apologized that time was tight and we couldn't have coffee with him. That moment, I felt an overwhelming desire to write down these stories before time could extinguish them." Ammi Hamdan responded, "As soon as the old folks die, those who have preserved their dishdashas, their songs, their dances, their stories about starvation, travels, and the death of their loved ones, their tasty dishes, their flavorful weddings and marriage rituals, the last open doors between us will collapse. If you can imagine, Amer, there are twenty thousand Omanis on the green island up until now and six thousand Omanis in Zanzibar according to one of my friends."

Jokha wondered, "Why aren't they given passports so that they can come back to their families, homes, farms, and neighborhoods? They can ask them for evidence, and we'd be able to confirm their Omani citizenship as soon as we see and hear them. They must know every inch of Oman as if they never left it for a moment. They must know its wells, sheikhs, tribes, and arts better than we do."

There was no answer in response to her emotional reaction, which took us all by surprise.

There was one lingering question that had been nagging at Ammi Hamdan, one that he deferred for a while and danced around by laughing and beating around the bush. I felt as if he was going to explode like a bomb if he didn't say it—if he did not allow it to get off his chest. Jokha listened in as she flipped through the TV channels. "Did Saeed see Bi Soura?" He asked. The tone of laughter and the playful mood shifted. Our eyes were now all on Amer. "Father, as I told you," Amer said. "He saw her only once. She was wearing a Biboy abaya and was heading toward the Umma party, the African political party that was loyal to the Omanis. That was the first and last time he saw her since the coup."

I felt both of their hearts sink, and I felt Jokha's curiosity. Amer added, a grimace on his face, "You know, father, what Saeed told me? He said I was too late to come searching for my mother, searching for my history and its story. That it was too late for me to write a novel about Zanzibar. The world around me spun that moment, and I felt as if I was going to fall and that that truth was choking me. Saeed clapped his hands and then threw them up in the air and said, 'everything has gone to its fate. Your mother, people, and history. Bah, it's over. Do you know the meaning of the word 'bah'?"

Ammi Hamdan wiped away his tears before we could see them. He muttered in a low voice, "Saeed is right. Saeed's right." Amer lost his usual poise. His voice grew louder as he said, "I took a walk with Saeed in the stone city that UNESCO adopted. He named each of the stone houses, one by one, according to their owners' names. There's the Maskari house, and there's the Riyami house . . .

I asked to see two graves, the grave of Abu Muslim al-Bahlani and the grave of Nasser Bin Abi Nabhan al-Kharusi, but I didn't see any graves. I wondered where their graves were. He told me, 'They've disappeared. They're lost.' I said, surprised, 'The Omani Consulate is completing its twentieth year in Zanzibar, and it hasn't been concerned about the grave of the iconic Omani poet Abu Muslim al-Bahlani or the grave of the scholar and philosopher al-Kharusi?'"

I don't know why the beautiful night had to end with such sudden anger. I don't know why Amer had thrown this bomb in his father's face. Ammi Hamdan kept his head down. Amer said goodbye to his mother and kissed his father's head and left. Was his novel messing with him? Was he upset that he had not found his mother where he expected to? I wasn't sure. I followed him. A small breeze of warm air made the sides of my open abaya flutter. I didn't want for our night—the night Jokha had laughed like that for the first time—to end that way. We got in the car. Amer's face was filled with a kind of anger and concern that I had never seen before. I decided that it was best to remain silent.

NIN19EEN

WE ENTERED our home. The clock pointed to two in the morning. I was overwhelmed by my longing for Amer, as if I was seeing him now after a long journey. Amer opened the door to his office. "I have a lot of things to do, Zahiyya," he said and then closed the door. My heart, my longing, stabbed at me, so I just staggered up to my room.

Amer didn't join me in bed. He slept in his office. It was one of the few times that he'd slept away from me when I was in the house. I was his nest. He would run after me, and I'd beat him by a step. The small distance remained a ploy to wake up the pleasure, a ploy for desire and resistance. I had not had enough of him, but he retreated far away. I wiped off my make-up with a special cleanser, sanitized my hands, hung my abaya on the rack, and put on my yellow cotton pajamas, giving up on the idea of wearing the red silk nightgown. I threw myself on the bed. I expelled my desire for Amer, his arms and kisses, and decided to surrender to my exhaustion and desire to sleep.

I repressed a gasp. The suicidal woman stood again in front of the painting I had made. She was shorter than the woman on the mural, and standing behind them, I was shorter than both of them. My heart beat rapidly, and I could not lift my heavy feet off the ground. I could not dislodge them, as if I were amidst moving sands. I was going to be held accountable for every step and breath. Where would I flee from her? She and I were suspended in a huge void. No earth beneath us, and no sky above. There was nothing I could cling to in order to save myself from her.

The suicidal woman suddenly decided to turn around. I watched her turn her face toward me. Electricity passed through my body, and I shivered. I warded the devil off with a prayer. I wanted to see her, and I didn't want to. I wanted to know her, and I didn't want to. I wanted to wake up from this nightmare of mine, and I didn't want to.

Blood froze in my veins. She had my angry eyes, my curled lips, my furrowed eyebrows. She had my grimacing face. It was me at the peak of my ugliness.

I woke up to the sound of my screaming, which emerged from a deep well within my soul. I turned on the light. I looked at my face in the mirror. Oh, God. I was uglier than I thought. I slapped my face until I was in pain. I shed tears, and then my wailing grew louder, like that of someone who had lost someone dear. The door to my room opened suddenly. Faneesh stood there, terrified. "I was cleaning nearby. The sound of your crying . . . " My anger and resentment grew. "How dare you break into my room?" I grabbed her hands. It was the first time I had ever gripped the arms of a maid. She seemed weak, fragile, depleted. "Madame, I swear to you, I entered the room because of your voice," she said. "I thought you needed help." I couldn't control my rapid breathing. My mouth was dry, my pulse accelerating. I let go of her and sat at the edge of the bed.

"Madame, your body is boiling. You're sweating," she said. "I'll go make something for..."

"Faneesh, tell me. What did you see in your last dream?"

"What dream?"

"The suicidal woman. What was your last dream?"

"I don't remember, Madame. I have many dreams."

I gripped her hands again. I asked her pleadingly, "Please, Faneesh, tell me." Faneesh escaped from my grip and left my room with the speed of a storm. Had she seen my own face too? What did that mean? Was I headed toward death? Could it be possible that I had been terrified of myself the past few months? Why did the woman have *my* face? Faneesh was not lying when she said that the suicidal woman had stolen her journal. She knew it was me, and she kept quiet about it.

I relaxed in the rocking chair for half an hour. I couldn't sleep, so I got up and washed my face with cold water. I kept on washing it until I thought it was going to vanish or transform. My face remained the same, but it was a little flushed. I brushed my teeth and dried my face well. I left my room and was met by the running woman, her head hanging from the ceiling. She looked different under the sunlight than she did under the neon lights at night. Was it possible that I had been painting myself on Raya and Yusuf's wall? I relaxed on the swing on the balcony, and a more brutal thought assaulted me. Was I going to die by suicide? Was I really going to throw myself from all the way up here? I shook off the thought, and chills ran through my entire body. But why would I commit suicide? I was a happy woman. I had a loving husband, a wonderful daughter, an amazing son. I had my own interests, I had my work, and I made good money. There was no convincing reason for me to commit suicide. There just wasn't. I took a deep breath and started to push away my negative thoughts as I repeated, "There is no convincing reason for suicide. There isn't." I grabbed the railing of the balcony. I was scared of falling down. I controlled myself and stepped down.

I looked at Amer, who was sleeping on the couch in the office. He was bareheaded, and he'd unbuttoned the dishdasha that he had worn to my in-laws' home the night before. I closed the door. I went into the kitchen that was filled with the smell of Faneesh's special coffee. My head was heavy with a headache. I sat at the table. Faneesh smiled nervously.

"Coffee, Madame?"

I nodded my head in agreement, so she handed me a warm cup that she poured out of the pot.

"Madame, I'm sorry. I prefer not to talk about my nightmares."

Her face was now close to mine. Her breathing accelerated as she set the coffee pot on the table.

"The dreams we talk about come true, Madame," she whispered in my ear. "Keep them in your heart. Endure their harm by yourself. Don't tell others your dreams."

Oh God, why was I here? Sitting here receiving advice from my maid? Listening to her great wisdom? Wasn't that a good enough reason to commit suicide? She had gotten me into her "square," locked me up behind doors and fences, and left the nightmare to guard me as it stood on top of my chest.

They were just superstitions, worthless superstitions that I shouldn't be buying into under any circumstances. I am exhausted, no more no less. I am confused. I will get over the dream, I will . . . my phone rang. It was Hind shaking with fear. Her voice quivering, she told me she had received a message about an Ethiopian maid who had hanged herself on the balcony of the house where she worked in Qaram early that morning. She was worried that it was Faneesh who had done that. I assured her that everything was fine. Hind thanked God over and over, and she told me to avoid conflict when dealing with servants.

I hung up the phone as I thought about the last thing she had said about the importance of avoiding conflict, since servants could not be trusted. These incidents happened all over the world. It was just a coincidence, no more. There were people who suddenly decided to end their lives, rich or poor, strong or weak, man or woman. When life loses its purpose, suicide becomes the easy, tough decision. We see it as ugly, while others see it as deliverance. They are free in their desires, but my life means a lot to me. My life is important. I want to preserve it. I want to live my life, one moment at a time. I don't want to be robbed of my time. Inner happiness washed over me, and I felt ecstatic as I thought about my future life opportunities. I increased the dosage of happy thoughts so that I could escape the ugliness of my nightmare. That I had seen my face did not mean that the suicidal woman was me. Maybe that was a prophetic sign about the suicide of the maid in the neighborhood. The idea appealed to me, and my frazzled nerves calmed a little.

Faneesh took my empty cup and poured me another one. I noticed her fingers as she put the coffee in my hands. They were dainty and soft, even though she scrubbed and washed my house daily. Her dark skin seemed shiny. She scurried away from me and drank her coffee while standing. I couldn't help myself from asking her with curiosity, "What kind of cream do you use for your hands?"

She looked at her hands nervously.

"Nothing, Madame. I don't use anything."

I almost touched her silky fingers to confirm what I saw. But I expelled the thought from my head. Faneesh got nervous, and her color changed.

"Does it bother you that I've been using the gelatin from the cactus tree?" she asked. "Mr. Amer doesn't mind."

"What are you talking about?"

"I mix the cactus gelatin with sugar and olive oil to moisturize my skin."

Why had she assumed I would get angry? Why was she worried about me learning her beauty secret? Every woman has her own recipe. She knew my recipe. I would cover my face with a rag, leaning over the vapors rising from boiling rice water so my pores could open up. She knew that I mixed sandalwood and yoghurt and put the concoction on my face before going to bed. She had told Amer about her recipe but hadn't told me. Was I the bogeyman or a monster?

Amer came in and interrupted my train of thought. He looked less eager, and a few droplets of water were scattered across his face. A forest of black hair jumped out of his unbuttoned dishdasha. He sat by my side. "Should I prepare something for you, boss?" Faneesh asked him. He asked to have some of her coffee, so she handed him a cup, smiling. I thought his arm was going to reach for mine, and that he was going to apologize for his coldness from the night before. My arm remained extended on the table, but his hand remained stuck to his forehead, like someone nursing a bad headache. The desire to reprimand him left my chest as soon as he said to me, "It was a legendary night, Zahiyya. I wrote until six in the morning."

"So, you didn't listen to Saeed al-Mahrouqi's advice?"

"What advice?"

"That the time for writing has passed."

"Quite the opposite," he said. "This is the time to write."

Amer guzzled the coffee. Then he raised his head in Faneesh's direction.

"Could you bring me some pastries and some milk tea with ginger to the office?"

He went back to his office. He slammed the door behind him forcefully. I gulped. He'd left me without another word, without suggesting that we have breakfast together, without drowning me in his fantastic stories that never ended. My heart raced as Faneesh was busy preparing his breakfast. Was that a good enough reason for suicide?

The barrage of dark thoughts burst in my soul again. Was Faneesh capturing Amer's heart behind my back? Was something growing between them as they tended to the garden and pruned it together once every two weeks, while I was busy drawing on sheilahs? Was Faneesh—with her dark color and pleasant nature and book reading—awakening Amer's special longing for Africa? I shook the evil thought from my head. It would be impossible for Amer to look at this nobody with anything more than just pity. I wasn't sure of anything, except for the fact that the second he'd come back to my home and lap, he seemed further away.

Faneesh prepared the food. I grabbed the tray from her hands and went to the office. Amer gave me half a glance. He gave me half a smile. I set the tray, somewhat nervously, on a small table next to the couch. With a voice that was closer to crying, I said, "What's going on with you, Amer?"

He got up from behind his desk, surprised.

"Zahiyya, what's the matter with you?"

We sat next to each other.

"You've changed."

Amer took a deep breath. He didn't kiss or hold me as he usually did whenever he noticed that I was angry or upset.

"Habibti, my dear, I took a vacation from work so I can write," he said. "I'm possessed with writing now. It's not as easy as you think."

Amer took out a recorder from the drawer. He said, "There are about nineteen hours of recordings on here, of stories about Omanis who lived in Africa. I need to get them out. Everything is merging in my head."

I controlled my desire to cry. "I don't want to bother you, but . . . "

Amer withdrew from me and leapt to his feet.

"All I want is time, Zahiyya."

I hid my tears as I walked away. I knew that time was not what Amer wanted. It was distance. Why did he want distance? I had never come in the way of his coming and going or the long hours he spent among his books, reading and traveling to the desert. The little time we had together was enough for me to get my fill of him, to forget the entire world around me. There were no closed doors between us. He would go out to the living room and make comments as I drew on the sheilahs, and I would come into his office and act mischievously—with a cup of ginger tea that I knew he couldn't resist—in order to distract him from his reading. He never used to read and write with that expressionless face, a face with no smile . . . and his body was never this lukewarm!

The moment I climbed up the stairs as I was headed to my room, I heard a strange sound coming from the kitchen. I took a few steps backwards. It was a ringing laughter that was flavored with tears. It was a voice filled with longing and eagerness, a language that I was hearing for the first time in my house. I was now across from the kitchen. Faneesh was pacing back and forth, with her back to me. She held the phone with one hand while the other rested on her thin waist. Her voice emerged with an unfamiliar zest. I didn't understand a word of what she said, but the sound of tears grew louder as she was about to finish her phone call. I had not realized that she had a voice until now. I had not realized that her voice had color, taste, and smell. The past few months, there was nothing between us except for a language that didn't belong to either one of us but was sufficient for giving orders and recommendations. Enough for communication.

Faneesh got scared as soon as she saw me near the door.

"I'm sorry, Madame," she said. "It's my family. I was just checking on my mother."

"How's her health now?"

"How did you know she's sick?"

"I didn't know she's sick," I said. "You said you called to check on her."

"She's at the hospital. The doctors said it's stomach cancer."

I hadn't talked to my mother for several months, and I hadn't visited my family. They didn't even notice my absence from their lives, and I didn't notice their absence from mine. My mother was only a few kilometers away, but I didn't miss her. The color of Faneesh's laughing, crying voice, as she was talking to her mother, brought back distant memories that I thought I had crossed out of my mind. I remembered my mother who had dressed me on the morning of Eid in a green dress with a piece of lace around the chest and lots of ruffles under the waist area. I didn't like the dress. It looked like something made for someone far older than me. I tried it more than once in my mother's room so I could talk myself into liking it, but I felt disappointed every time.

My mother insisted on parting my hair in the middle and pulling it in the back. I screamed in her face, "I don't want an old woman's hairdo!" My mother got angry, slapped me on the face, and wrapped my little body between her legs. She started putting a huge amount of coconut oil in my hair. She combed my hair with reckless anger, as I cried out loud. She pulled my hair back with all the power she could muster, until the oil started running down my forehead, cold, and the veins on my head tightened up and turned incredibly green. She put a string around my thick hair that she had cut out of one her headscarves.

The girls strutted around in their dresses and carried purses stuffed with Eid money. They rushed to the Eid souqs, where they bought toys and sweets, while I stayed in our backyard crying as I attempted nonstop to untie the damn string. All I had wanted was to wear my long black hair down my back without oil or cream. But my mother had always wanted me to wear my hair like hers, to dress like her, and to talk like her.

"Where did you talk to your family before?" I asked Faneesh.

"In my room," she said. "I promise this will be the last time I talk in the kitchen."

"Is your mother going to be alright?"

"I hope so," she said. "I sent them all the money I have so she could get a good treatment."

I didn't say anything else. Sadness gnawed at my heart and led me to a point of no return. I went up the stairs. I tried to recall nice things that my mother had done for me. Nice things that my father had done for me. But the only things that leapt in the vicinity of my memory were their frowning faces, their constant fear of things that didn't even happen. My father worked on polishing his reputation every day. My father's reputation was his capital in life, and my mother was possessed by her husband's approval, which she associated with the approval of God and his angels. The world spun around me. Who do I tell my story to? Who do I open up to about the anguish that inhabited me now? I called Tarfa and asked her to go out with me. She was surprised.

"You don't even go out when Amer is traveling. How come you want to go out when he's at home?"

"I'm suffocating, Tarfa."

The world seemed strange to me every time I went out by myself. I always felt extremely nervous. My heart would start racing. I couldn't stop looking around as if I was being chased by some unknown people. I left the house without putting on any makeup or lipstick. The big sunglasses, which covered up a large part of my face, made me feel a bit more relaxed and safe.

I arrived at the Starbucks in Jawharat al-Shati, where we had agreed to meet. I parked the car in the parking lot. A sweaty Indian man in dirty clothes appeared in front of me. His hair, which reeked of the smell of coconut oil, reminded me of my childhood hair. He smiled at me. "Madame, you want me to clean the car?" he asked. I didn't know what grave he had emerged out of. I didn't know from what hell he had borrowed his smile. I had always passed by without noticing them or hearing their words. I would pass, as if they were not even there, as if they had no voice, no words, and no smell. I took a chance, approaching so that I could smell him—as if he were a creature who had just landed from outer space. He did not stink like I had expected. The Indian's smile shrank. I scrutinized his face, his cracked hands, and his fingernails, where black dirt had squeezed deep under. He was startled by me. "So, Madame, I clean the car?" he asked. I nodded my head in agreement.

That was not me. That was not my nature. Those were not my habits. How could I have allowed this dirty idiot to clean my car? I couldn't turn around to see him. I worried I'd throw up if I did. He was not the only one I saw. Suddenly, I saw many like him. One of them inserted the fuel hose in the car's tank, and another one smiled as I passed by a store where he worked. A third one carried a huge rice sack on his head and then put it in a red pickup truck, before grabbing half a riyal from the hand of the man sitting in the car.

Strange noises grew louder up in the sky, so I raised my head to find an uncountable number of them busy building an enormous mall. One of them opened the door to Starbucks for me and gestured for me to come inside. Where had they been hiding? Why hadn't I seen their smiles, colors, and voices? I was terrified. Was this happening to me because I was about to die? I had heard my grandmother say, "A person senses when he's about to die and sees things he didn't use to see."

Tarfa had gotten there before I did. She motioned for me to join her. She kissed me, and we sat down. She asked me slyly about Amer's return and our feverish reunion. I slapped her wrist so she would stop joking about these things. I told the waiter I wanted a sealed bottle of water. Tarfa asked for an orange juice.

When the waiter left, she said to me, "Your face looks tired. Your situation is difficult. Is it the maid again?"

"No, it's about Amer."

"Khayr Inshallah, is everything OK?"

"Amer is stressed out and irritated. He hasn't said much since being back."

"Bismillah, Praise God," she said. "You two are the most beautiful couple in the world, and your life is like milk and honey."

"Amer wants time and space . . . he says he wants to write."

"Zahiyya, I don't like the state you're in," she said. "This whole thing about dreams and stories of suicide, and now you are telling me that Amer has changed. I say fire her and be done with it."

"What are you talking about?"

"Habibti, my dear. This Faneesh woman has cast a spell on you two. What's happening to you guys is not normal."

I wanted to open my mouth to say something, but I didn't say anything. The waiter put the bottle of water in front of me. Tarfa wasn't going to understand what I had come to say. I would not have understood either.

"Zahiyya, I'm on pins and needles. What's the matter with you?"

Tarfa unleashed a barrage of questions. I felt as if I couldn't hear her—as if a sound barrier suddenly stood between us. She kept on talking and talking, while I was in a different part of the world. I realized something that had escaped my mind. Amer had been looking for his mother in me. His mother was never in Africa. I am his mother. Africa was nothing but material for a story conjured up by people who passed through it. Amer loved me as I baked Omani bread and prepared shorbat al-habb, makbous, and kabouli for him the way kids loved their mothers' home-cooked meals. He loved me as I fed him with my hands. He loved the way I cradled his body close to mine, the way mothers cradle their infants, more so than those moments we were fused as lovers. He loved my touch on his forehead when he was suffering from a headache and asked me to give him some medicine and rub some stinky Vicks ointment on his chest and back. Raya and Yusuf grew up, but Amer remained my spoiled child. Amer knows that his mother will not come back, that she will not awaken from her absence. Quite simply, he is satisfied with me.

I stood up. I almost screamed, "I got it!" I grabbed my purse and said suddenly, "Tarfa, I have to go. I'm sorry."

"What about lunch and stories?"

"I don't think I should leave Amer. He hasn't had anything to eat."

I rushed out of the restaurant, as if happiness were pushing me forward. I sensed a little victory in my chest. The Indian stood smiling near my black Mercedes. My car looked sparkly and clean. I asked him, "How much?" He said, "One and a half riyals." I handed him two riyals so that he could keep the rest for himself. He bent over my window. "Thank you, Madame. Would you like a Nawras?" he asked, taking a stack of recharge cards out of his pocket. I bought a Nawras card for five riyals even though I didn't use these prepaid phone cards. I have a regular phone line. I asked him, "What's your name?" His smile widened, and I saw his two rotting teeth as he said, "Santosh."

I don't know why I had allowed him to wash my car! I don't know why I had bought a card from him. Did I pity him or what? All I knew for sure was that I didn't want for Santosh to lose his smile. My girlfriends had told me about street vendors, car cleaners, garbage men, and bathroom janitors at malls, parks, and restaurants, but the very rare times I had left my house, I had never seen them. Santosh was the first man I had ever seen or talked to among them.

I returned home. I made mulukhiyya the way I had learned how to cook it in Egypt. I set up the table. I gently knocked on Amer's door.

"Habibi, my darling. Shall we eat?"

"Sure. God, I'm starving!"

We sat next to each other, and Amer dug into his food without saying a word.

"You look exhausted."

"I'm in a state of emergency."

"Okay, tell me a little about your writing."

His face lit up with childlike enthusiasm, and he started talking. I besieged him with my attention. I asked him attentively about the stories of people who had been keeping him away from me. He pressed on my hands with tenderness and said, "I love the mulukhiyya, Zahiyya." My heart fluttered like a small bird who'd gotten wet in the rain. Amer had regained his face. Oh my, what writing had been doing to him! It almost transformed him into a man I didn't recognize.

"Habibi, I appreciate what you're doing," I said.

He patted my back affectionately. "That's all I want."

I fed him a bite of mulukhiyya with my hand, after wrapping it in a piece of Lebanese bread.

"You've been a little on edge, right?"

He swallowed the bite.

"I'm writing now about something brutal, Zahiyya," he said. "I'm writing about the slave market that Saeed al-Mahrouqi took me to."

I was surprised. "Slave market?"

Amer reclined in his chair.

"I found myself inside a Portuguese fortress that very much resembled the fortresses in Oman. I saw an oval shaped amphitheater in the middle of the fortress. The horrific statues shocked me. The hair on my hands stood up. The statues were of children, men, and women bound in chains. Their faces were fraught with sadness and sorrow. I saw in their eyes that something was awaiting them. A dark fate and hazy stories. I asked Saeed apprehensively, 'where are we?' and he said to me, 'We're in the biggest slave market in Africa.' I didn't say anything, while the world spun around me. If you can imagine, Zahiyya, there were underground rooms in which they put around 175 male and female slaves! They would weaken them so they wouldn't resist the men flogging them. Some of the men were castrated. Many of them had to endure the ugliest of pains so that they may be sold for a high price, and the weak ones would return to their rooms again. I put my head in my hands because of what I saw, Zahiyya. The statues stared at me. Some artist had created them to make our hearts ache every time we passed by there. Arabs used to buy some of those slaves, and they treated them as part of a deal."

My skin crawled as I imagined 175 people in the same room. I could tell Amer was angry from his facial expressions. He looked like he was about to say something but then refrained from saying it.

"I read that Sayyid Bargash Bin Said was among the first people who became involved in abolishing the slave trade in Zanzibar."

Faneesh took away the dishes and put in front of us a plate of rahash cubes sprinkled with nuts, alongside a pot of coffee and some cups.

"Before Saeed and I parted, he handed me a book titled *The Slave Community*. The main value of the book lies in the fact that it was written from the perspective of the enslaved."

I opened my ears well to Amer's stories. He said many things that I didn't understand, but I was happy because I was now closer to him. I could hear his voice and laughter, feel his warmth, and shrink the distance to his heart.

TW20TY

I FORGOT THE phone card that I had bought from Santosh for days in my purse, and when I opened the purse to grab my phone, I found it. I summoned Faneesh and asked her, "Are you still using the Nawras card that I gave you when you first arrived here?" Surprised, she responded with a "yes."

"I bought you a recharge card so you can check on your mother."

She looked at me with tremendous surprise, extended her hand, and grabbed the card.

"That's very generous of you, Madame."

I went up to my room, as a big burden was lifted off my shoulders. I climbed the stairs, feeling light, and wanting to jump in the air. A safe distance had extended between me and my fears. I remembered that I had wasted away my university years hiding in the hole of my soul and that I didn't know anything about Egypt, except for my one friend, her father, and her home. I didn't dare venture into its streets and crowded busses. I didn't have the courage to smile at the man who sold fava beans from a cart close to our apartment. I didn't walk by the Nile on moonlit nights, and I didn't go to Giza to look at the pyramids. Four years passed, as I swaddled myself with endless plans to create safety and concocted ways to disguise myself like a lizard. If anybody ever asked me what I remember about Egypt, I couldn't tell them about anything except for the black-and-white films that I watched on TV I never went to the cinema once, even though I was in the "mother of the world." I am terrified of places that are crowded with people. I lose my balance in them. I lose my ability to focus, and I look like someone who is about to go into a coma.

I reached the second floor and took a look at the hanged woman who was swimming in endless memories. I tried to look for a resemblance between us. But she didn't look like me at all. I turned my back to her and kept on walking. But something made me look at her again. My heart started beating harder. I saw her raise her hands and pull her long hair away from her face. She gave me the look that I knew very well. That serious, stern look that was full of orders and warnings and fear from me and for me. I left her behind me and ran to my room. How had my mother's face emerged from under her thick hair? How had she trapped me with the net of her look, the look that I had grown tired of running away from? If I had remained standing before her for any longer, she would have showered me with her eternal wrath for something I did not know and had not yet discovered.

Amer came in and noticed my sadness and anxiety. He caressed my fingertips.

"I know my being busy is taking a toll on you," he said. "But since I've made some progress on my writing, what do you think of inviting the guys to a barbecue?"

I was delighted. I needed something to pull me out of the vortex of my thoughts that bred endless concerns. I called Hind and Tarfa, and Amer called their husbands Khaled and Rashed, and they welcomed the invitation.

Amer and I went out to buy supplies for the barbecue. I carefully read the instructions about the products more than once. Amer almost lost his mind, but that's my style. I don't buy anything before reading everything written on it, in big or small print—production date, expiration date, and natural and artificial ingredients. I learned to be prudent ever since I traveled abroad and started to shop by myself. Amer said to me jokingly, "My blood pressure has gone up!" But it was my nature that made the shopping trip special. I bought what I wanted, and we went back home.

I put on gloves and started preparing my special spice mix that gave the barbecue an irresistible flavor. Faneesh stood making the salad and watching me from time to time. I called for her, and she approached me, happy.

"Do you want to learn my special recipe?"

She nodded her head yes.

"By the way, I rarely give anyone my secrets."

Her smile widened more as she dried her hand with a rag.

"Watch me closely," I said. "I make the spice rub with garlic, vinegar, salt, turmeric, and red pepper, and I then add to it some tamarind with barbecue sauce and yoghurt."

Faneesh jotted down the ingredients in her little notebook. She watched me as I turned the meat cubes in the spice rub a few times. I noticed her giving me a strange look. A look I wasn't used to. In a tone that wasn't sharp, I said, "What is it, Faneesh?"

She seemed hesitant as she shifted her gaze between looking at my hands, which were still seasoning the meat pieces, and my eyes.

"I'm sorry, Madame," she said. "It just occurred to me . . . "

The movement of my hands stopped.

"What?"

She became more silent and shy. I noticed that Faneesh had a special kind of beauty. Her narrow eyes had thick lashes, and her straight brows didn't need any waxing. Her thin face featured pronounced cheekbones, and her smile revealed a small dimple on the left side. Her shyness turned into a soft blush that made her features even daintier.

"Madame, there's something I really like about you," she said.

I didn't say anything as I noticed how deep her dark eyes were.

"It amazes me how you cook as if you're painting," she said. "You walk, talk, and get upset as if you're actually painting."

I couldn't find the right words to respond to her, and I felt embarrassed. Amer came in and attacked the salad platter.

I told him playfully, "make sure you leave some for the guests."

Faneesh left. I took off the gloves and tossed them in the trash. I closed the lid of the meat container so it would better soak up the seasoning. Amer approached me.

"What's going on?" he said.

He swallowed the slice of cucumber that was in his hand and resumed talking. "I feel like something is different between you and Faneesh."

I came closer to him. "And that's not good?"

He burst out laughing. "It's good. It's better than good, wallah, I swear."

I sat next to Amer at the kitchen table.

"I don't know where to start, Amer," I said. "There are many things that I haven't told you about me. You haven't asked me about them, although you've seen and lived these things with me. Maybe you've felt them throughout the years we've been married, but you prefer to overlook them."

I was about to cry.

"Do you know, Amer, why I love you more than anything?"

His face lit up.

"Because you're the only one who overlooks my mistakes. I was held responsible for my mother's mistakes. Responsible for my father's mistakes. But you, you don't see my mistakes. You see Zahiyya."

He extended his hands and took mine in his. I resisted my tears.

"I used to worry about every big and small detail. I worried about what I said, my mannerisms, my clothes, my germs, my snot, my dandruff, and the dirt on my shoes. I worried about people's reactions around me whenever I avoided shaking their hands and hugging them. I hated all my female relatives who would kiss me, and I felt like killing them. I shut myself behind doors during holidays and special occasions, and I deprived myself of receiving Eid money. Amer, did you know that I never quit reminiscing, opening up these folders of mine, one after the other, before going to sleep? It's like I get pleasure from recalling all my mistakes and replaying them on the screen of my memory. I remember the night I cried for a long time because I'd dropped my box of watercolors in class, and the paint pans got scattered all over the classroom. I tried to pick them up more than once, but I couldn't. My hands resisted doing that. My heart trembled. My evil mind told me all about the germs and dirt that had walked all over the colors. One of my classmates said, 'the jinn for sure doesn't lick colors . . . just pick them up.' She and the other girls in class burst out laughing. I repressed my anger and saved it until I returned home, locked myself up in my room, and cried. I would scold myself out of fear of forgetting my schoolbooks. Out of fear of not knowing the answers on a test. Out of fear that my table or the chair I was sitting on was dirty. I would scold myself before my mother scolded me over housework, cooking, and cleaning, and before my father's long cane made its way to my back. All that scolding took over my happiness, Amer. But your embrace saved me. It lessened my vicious, fatal thoughts. You won't believe it, but during my many bouts of depression, I contemplated suicide. But I never dared do it, despite coming up with detailed plans."

Amer's face tightened, and he looked more serious. "Zahiyya, I don't like to hear this kind of talk at all." I became anxious, and I felt the need to keep him beside me, to keep the warmth of his hands in mine.

"My problems subsided when I gathered up the courage to travel to Egypt and face life on my own. They subsided even more when we got married. I'm fine when I'm with you. I am changing. Amer, I'm not afraid of Faneesh anymore."

Amer's eyebrows were furrowed in surprise.

"Were you ever afraid of her?" he asked. "You've been the reason behind every maid's terror."

I took a deep breath.

"I was defending myself. I would scream and ask for impossible things and confront them with an angry, sullen, and depressed face from the early morning, so they would tread carefully. I was scared of them poisoning me, which is why I did all the cooking myself. I was scared of their smells, their sticky bodies. I would imprison them in the "square" to weaken them, and I would whip them with lashes of anger and instruction. The ones who behaved would stay, and the ones who turned into 'afreeta demons would leave my "square" and my house forever."

Still apprehensive, Amer watched me as he waited for me to say more.

HUDA HAMED

"What happened, Zahiyya?"

I grabbed a tissue and wiped off the tears that swelled in my eyes.

"What I know for sure is that the sides of the square have cracked open."

We both got quiet and didn't have anything to say to each other.

"Is that what the dream is about, Amer?"

He reclined backwards.

"I don't believe in dreams, Zahiyya," he said. "I think it's you. It's you overcoming yourself and your fears."

My face lit up. I almost threw myself into his lap.

"Zahiyya, I have something to ask of you."

I was now closer to his face, his breath.

"Your mother and father, try to remember something nice about them," he said.

I pulled my hand from his. My pulse raced, and an angry chill ran through my body. I left him and climbed up the stairs, but as soon as I got to the top, I went back down. I climbed the stairs and then came back down again. I repeated that once, twice, and ten times. Here I was, repeating my actions, counting the stairs again, afraid that they might be missing a step. It was as if I was scared of miscounting, as if I was running with the suicidal woman. But I *was* the suicidal woman!

And now, what could I remember about my parents? They had no virtues. I went up and down. My heart was going to stop. My breath grew louder. My memory opened up its old notebook. They had no virtues. I went up and down. I collided with Amer's body. He embraced me tightly. He halted my movement. He fell down from the force of our collision, and I fell on top of him. I breathed hard. The air came out of my lungs, hot. I felt my heart about to leave my chest. I cried. I shed a lot of tears over Amer's dishdasha. The two of them have no virtues, Amer. No virtues!

Amer pulled me into his lap. He patted my back. He absorbed the energy of my anger. All of my anger. As if nothing had happened. He smiled at me, brushing the short strands of hair away from my face.

"We don't want to ruin the barbecue."

My breath calmed down. I regained my strength. He got up, pulling me with him.

"Give yourself a chance, Zahiyya."

TWEN21Y ONE

WE SAT IN the courtyard. We took out the grilling supplies. The white plastic table and chairs. Amer fired up the coals. I gazed at my garden, which was surrounded by colorful lights and the sound of water dancing in the fountain. I recalled my constant desire to pull up Amer's trees, one tree after another. It was the first time I ever saw the garden look so beautiful. For the first time, I wasn't provoked by the thought that the trees were filled with insects, attracting snakes and mice.

Hind, Tarfa, Khaled, and Rashed arrived. Hind and Tarfa joined me. Rashed and Khaled rushed to help Amer and got entangled in long conversations about Zanzibar and the trip that had turned into a writing project. Hind, Tarfa, and I recalled our school days. The three of us had attended the first girls' school that opened in al-Batina. We met each other in junior high. Tarfa had completed elementary school in Muscat after her father had returned from Zanzibar, and Hind had gone to elementary school in Bahrain, where her father had studied, worked, and had kids. Then fate decided that we would be at the same school. Tarfa said, "Zahiyya, you were among the first girls from al-Batina who received an education, and your father gets credit for that."

Not all the families welcomed the idea of educating their daughters as much as they welcomed educating their sons, since educating boys meant employment, whereas educating girls brought about scandal, as my mother used to say. Oh, how many girls of my generation had stayed at home or gone to school for a little while before withdrawing into early matrimony. In his entire life, my father had left Oman only twice. He'd gone to Saudi Arabia, once to perform the 'Umra and once to perform the Hajj. My mother told him repeatedly that a girl belonged to the kitchen, her husband, and the grave, but my father insisted that I go to school. Of course, he did that because the al-Kayumi daughter wasn't less important than the sheikhs' daughters who had gone to school. Whenever my father saw me make good grades and study diligently, he would encourage me to make him even more proud, whereas my mother complained that I wasn't cleaning the house or cooking like the neighbors' daughters who stayed at home. I imagine what my life would have been like if I hadn't gone to school. If I had gotten married at sixteen and kept on having a baby every two years. Oh my God, a crazy idea and a depressing life for sure. My father wasn't opposed to the idea that I was going to be the first girl to leave the village for Egypt, even if he had done that just to please the sheikhs. He would send me a good monthly allowance and letters to check on me while I was there. But why was I overlooking all that and just remembering the purple bruise on my back?

Faneesh set the fruit, plates, and a basket of bread on the table. When Faneesh left, Tarfa and Hind asked me if "the spell was broken or not." I didn't like them whispering behind Faneesh's back. Hind said, "Listen, I've always said that a maid is part of the family, and that we should treat them like human beings. But this theory is not true at all. You're right, Zahiyya. We have to be strict with them, or else they'd walk all over us. My maid Nathalie threatens to leave every day over the stupidest thing." Tarfa said, "And I, after all my experiences, I never got anywhere. I say, you're right Zahiyya. Imagine that before Nancy's departure, Khaled told me to search her belongings, but I refused. I said this honest woman had taken care of my home for four years. But after Khaled insisted, I went ahead and searched. I didn't find anything at first. But the shampoo bottle was making a strange noise. I poured out the shampoo in the sink, and there it was, a bunch of gold! Bracelets and a necklace and earrings." Hind said, "Speaking of gold, check out the diamond set that Rashed gave me as a gift for our anniversary a couple of days ago." Hind raised her sheilah to reveal a beautiful diamond necklace, and as she released her ears from under it, the sparkling diamonds in her ears looked stunning in the moonlight. She extended her arm to show us the remaining part of the set, a ring whose diamond sparkled like a star in the sky. I said to her, "Rashed has great taste, wallah." Tarfa said in a loud voice, "Poor me, no one gives me gifts of gold, let alone diamonds." We all laughed, and Khaled said jokingly, "No one told you to marry a poor man!"

We were surrounded by the delicious smell of grilled meat as Amer unloaded the skewers on our plates. We quickly got up, one after the other, to wash our hands in the hall inside before returning to eat—with a big appetite—and chat about work, politics, and art. Rashed said, "It's been a while, Zahiyya, since you've done any artwork." Khaled swallowed the bite in his mouth. "That's true. It's been years since we saw your last piece." Tarfa laughed, "Man, the woman is busy with her business. She doesn't have any time for art." Her words hurt my feelings. "That's not true," I said. Tarfa could tell I was upset. "Zahiyya, I'm just kidding! But it's true. Painting on sheilahs and designing abayas have been taking up all of your time."

Amer scooped up more salad onto my plate, as if telling me not to get upset. "I don't have an idea for a painting," I said. Hind said, "There are plenty of ideas out there." My voice became sharper as I said, "I want a subject that moves something inside me."

Amer looked at me, and everybody stopped talking. "I agree with Zahiyya," he said "For many years, I had the idea to write about Zanzibar. It was an old idea, but I needed the impetus to write it. I needed motivation, a repertoire of knowledge, energy, and time." Rashed took a sip from the orange juice glass that Faneesh had left by his side, as she did for the rest of us. "I see this issue from a different perspective," he said. "I mean, Zahiyya, you should go find your topics. There are no guarantees that they are going to come to you." I nodded in agreement. "You're right," I said. "But as Amer said, I don't have any motivation or desire to draw now."

I got up from the dinner table and brought the notebook that had my new designs. It was a new project, one that completely differed from my old designs that were filled with loud colors and gems and luxury. The new designs were dainty, simple designs with a touch of African style. I flipped through the pages in front of them, as if defending myself— that I was doing something, that something was keeping me busy.

Hind said, "This is far from your taste." Tarfa said, "Is this about change?" I was surprised by their cold reaction. "You don't like them?" They agreed that they were different, but no one said they were nice.

Khaled changed the subject. "We're talking about the other kind of art. We're worried you're going to forget about it, Zahiyya." The bitter truth they were talking about stabbed at me. But what could I draw? My previous works were about my obsessions, fears, and challenges. I no longer wanted to work in that space fraught with landmines, fears, and agitation. Painting on sheilahs and designing abayas made me a woman who created beauty—who made wedding and birthday cakes for the soul.

Hind's voice grew louder as she yelled out my name from inside the house. Tarfa and I got up and went to her. "Zahiyya, I can't find my diamond ring," she said as she pointed to the sink nervously. "I took it off here to wash my hands before we ate, and I forgot to put it back on." I was troubled. I rushed like a mad woman to look for it on top of the sink and under it. I looked for it inside the bathroom, near the chairs in the hall and behind them. Tarfa helped me look. "Try to remember, where did you put it?" I asked. She answered me in a loud, angry voice, "I'm sure I took it off here and forgot to put it back on." My head started to spin. Tarfa said, "OK, where did it go then?"

Faneesh came out to collect the dirty dishes from the table. Hind called out to her, screaming, "Hey . . . you!" Faneesh turned around, surprised. She put her index finger on her chest and asked, "Me?" She rushed to us. "You took the ring from here," Hind said, pointing to the sink again. Faneesh understood what Hind was saying. "No, Madame," she said. Hind became more on edge. "If you didn't take it, then who did . . . the jinn?" Faneesh became nervous. I could almost hear her heartbeats, but she kept her silence. "Listen, if you don't get the ring immediately, this will be your last day here. Got it?" Faneesh kept her composure. "You're sitting here looking at me? I said get the ring now."

Faneesh's voice grew loud for the first time since she had entered my house. She said in English, "Just because you lost your ring doesn't mean I stole it." She withdrew and ran toward her room. Tarfa was angry, "Daughter of . . . a maid talking back?" My heart squeezed with pain, as if I were the one being humiliated. My voice got stuck, and I couldn't say anything. Hind turned to me and said, "Clearly, your maid is a thief."

"I think it's better for us to search her room before making any judgements," Tarfa said.

Amer, Khaled, and Rashed came to us and asked what was going on, having heard our loud voices. Hind talked about her missing ring. Rashed got angry at her for not taking care of her valuables. He chastised her in front of us. She was about to cry. "How is it my fault that their maid is a thief?" Amer's face welled up with anger. He couldn't restrain himself. "Hind, you better show some self-respect." Amer's sentence struck us like a lightning bolt. Khaled said, "Now we're fighting over a maid." Rashed said, "Hind is the one to blame. We're really sorry." Hind stood up like she was a different woman, one that I didn't recognize. "I'm going to go search her room now, and I'm definitely going to find it," she said. I don't know how I gripped her hand tightly. "You will not go search her room. I won't allow you to do that." Hind froze. "Are you defending this trash, Zahiyya? Your maid, the reason for your misery, dreams, and sickness?"

Hind walked away, loaded with anger and agitation. She went out to the courtyard. We all went out behind her. As soon as she yanked her purse off the table, we all heard the sound of something hitting the floor. Something sparkled like a star in the sky.

TWEN**22** TWO

THE PARTY BROKE UP before the fruit and platter of sweets that I had prepared were eaten. Hind left, almost unable to look at us, because of how embarrassed she was. Rashed apologized to us repeatedly. Tarfa and Khaled also withdrew in cold silence. Amer and I sat down. We had nothing to say to each other. We contemplated the sky and listened to the sound of the water circulating in the fountain, as if we had agreed in silence not to discuss what had happened.

"I remembered something nice about my father today," I said.

Amer smiled at me and pressed on my fingers.

"And tomorrow you'll remember nicer things about your mother."

He patted my shoulders. "I'll help you clean up."

Amer cleaned the grill. I carried the plates inside, emptied the remaining food, and washed them.

"I'll be in my office for a couple of hours, and then I'll follow you, beautiful," Amer said. "Don't go to sleep."

I smiled at him in agreement.

I went to Faneesh's room. I knocked at the door. She opened the door and met me, her eyes red.

"I'm sorry, Madame," she said. "I'll finish the cleaning now."

She wiped her tears away with the sleeve of her pajama. I went into her room. I sat on the side of her bed.

"You can search the room," she said. "Search my bags. My closet. My clothes. I'm not a thief."

Faneesh's voice was loud, and she moved her hands more quickly than she spoke. She wiped the fluids from her nose by pressing on it with her thumb and index finger. Faneesh pulled her suitcase from under her bed. Her face turning into a grimace, she rummaged through her belongings and then opened her closet.

"Go ahead and search it. Search over here too."

I remained calm, giving her the opportunity to cry and rummage through her things.

"Faneesh, I came to say that I believe you."

Her crying subsided. A look of surprise appeared on her face. Her raging anger subsided. I was about to leave her room when she said, "Madame . . . "

She gulped as I turned to look at her.

"In the last dream, I saw your face."

I felt an electric current run through my body. Faneesh sat down and cried. Her face became childlike. Her long lashes turned into umbrellas, wet with the rain of her tears. I approached her.

"That doesn't make me sad, Faneesh."

She raised her head. I was now close to her. My mind sent me warning messages about not getting closer. My hand perched on her soft shoulders. My fear, disgust, and nervousness withdrew through another window in my soul.

"Faneesh, I want to ask you for something."

Faneesh was startled. She was surprised, for here I was in her room sitting on the side of her bed. She backed away.

"I want to draw you."

The questions leapt from her eyes like tigers.

"Draw me?"

I smiled at her.

"Yes, and I'll pay you a fee."

Her face lit up. She looked assured and nodded in agreement.

TWEN**23**THREE

A LONG TIME had passed since I had gone up to the art studio, the room that stood above the second floor. Faneesh would clean it once a week and then give me the key so that I could put it with the others. I studied my covered paintings and then unveiled some of them. I had mixed feelings at that moment. I sat in a chair and put my elbows on the table. I took out a piece of paper and sketched Faneesh's face. I divided the paper up into four squares. In the first square, Faneesh's face was expressionless. In the second square, her hair was neatly tucked under a white scarf, and she had her work face on. The serious look on her face and her smile were based on specific, rigid measurements. In the third square, I drew her with disheveled hair and an angry face—she looked like she was about to cry. In the fourth square, she was laughing. Her mouth was open, her eyes narrowed. I looked at the paper on which I had sketched Faneesh from different angles. I didn't like what I had drawn. Oh, my God. I no longer wanted to draw her inside these squares. Faneesh had to leave the square. An idea flashed in my head. I wrote on another piece of paper, "Faneesh leaving the square means that I should go out with her." I tore up the drawing. I had to think of something else. But what could it be?

I left the studio. I went down the stairs. The hanged woman met me, and before I turned around to get away from her, she pulled her hair up again and showed me my mother's face smiling with tenderness and overwhelming fear. I had no memory of that smile. When had my mother smiled at me like that? I couldn't remember. I couldn't remember at all. I shook my head. The face almost ripped itself from the wall and ran after me. I ran to my room, locked the door with the key, and leaned my back to the door, afraid that the ghost of the face would follow me.

I closed my eyes, tearing up. I had seen my mother with that exact face when they lifted me out of the farm's pond, where I had almost drowned. They'd pressed on my chest to expel the water that impeded my breathing. She had that same face when I contracted malaria in my early childhood. The doctor had told her that my survival was impossible. I cried more as I saw her in my memory with that same face as she hugged me at al-Seeb Airport when I returned from Egypt, with my big diploma. She had the same face when she held Raya in her arms for the first time and sang to her, "*Bubble up coffee pot, bubble up coffee pot. Raya, you torture me with your love, you make my heart melt.*" I couldn't repress my desire to cry and burst open like a water balloon. Amer knocked on the door after realizing that it was locked from the inside, so I opened the door for him and buried myself in his chest. I cried. He held my face between his hands.

"What's wrong, Zahiyya?"

I buried my head in his chest again. He sat me on a chair.

"Are you crying because you can't draw or what?"

I grabbed some tissues and wiped my eyes and nose.

"I'm tired, and I want to go to sleep."

We didn't talk, Amer and I. We slept in each other's arms.

TWEN**24** FOUR

FANEESH PUT ON her blue uniform, wrapped her hair in a white scarf, and got ready for the mission.

"Madame, I'm ready."

I studied her clothes and shook my head.

"You don't like my clothes?"

I laughed as I fidgeted with the car keys between my fingers.

"Faneesh, just put on your regular clothes. Dress like the Ethiopian Christian girl who used to go for walks in the fields of Addis Ababa, or the young woman who used to walk in the university hallways."

Faneesh was shocked. She remained sullen, not understanding what I was saying.

"We're going out together," I said. "We'll take a walk in Muscat, go shopping, and have ice cream at Baskin Robbins, and then we'll go see a movie in the evening."

Faneesh was disappointed.

"I don't understand, Madame," she said. "You're not going to draw me?"

I laughed and said to her, "I'm not going to make you stand for hours in front of me so that I can draw you. I want to see you, Faneesh, so that I can know how to draw you."

Faneesh and I went out. I asked her to sit in the passenger seat next to me. She had put on a pair of jeans and a loose, long-sleeved white shirt which she'd buttoned all the way up. She left her tied hair open to the wind and sun.

"Can I go out like this in Oman?"

I smiled at her.

"Today is an exception."

I felt safe. I crossed the street, and not for a second did I worry that the people driving next to me, in front of me, or behind me were busy watching me as I had always thought. Faneesh also let go of her anxiety and started talking about random things and laughing. We walked next to each other. Many men, women, children, and laborers passed by us, but their bodies were not scary or overwhelming. We sat in Baskin Robbins near al-Noor Hall and ordered ice cream.

"This is one of the rare times I've eaten outside the home, Faneesh."

I enjoyed the strawberry and vanilla ice cream, and I didn't think about whether or not the Filipino had been wearing gloves. I didn't think about whether or not his nails were cut. I didn't care if his moustache was trimmed or if the hair on his head was covered or shaved. In fact, I forgot what the Filipino looked like as soon as I sat down and started eating the delicious ice cream. My obsessions retreated from my chest, like snakes crawling away on a rainy night when the seasons are changing.

I couldn't tell exactly what was happening to me. All I knew was that I was less fearful and more joyful. Did I need my maid to hold my hand so I could have the courage to face life? We went to the al-Shati' Cinema. We watched the American film *Life of Pi*, which is based on Yann Martel's novel. I thought of Amer as I saw the Canadian novelist visiting Pi, the Indian man, in his house so that he could have a story to write, like Amer had visited Saeed al-Mahrouqi to get the stories of Zanzibar. I was surprised by how the protagonist's name, "Pi," had been transformed in meaning from a beautiful swimming pool to a dirty Indian bathroom, and how he'd become a laughingstock. I watched how the children laughed at him and recalled how the girls in class had also laughed at me for completely different reasons, but I was sure that my feelings were similar to Pi's. Pi searched for God in his own religion and in other religions and got lost amongst them, just like Faneesh had gotten lost between her religion and the one that Hajjah Moudi had suggested for her. The ship got wrecked, and Pi survived, only to face all sorts of dangers at sea, where dreams merged with reality. Pi survived like I had survived secret and constant suicide attempts—none of which I had come close to executing. Pi wrote his memoirs daily, in defense of his existence and his life in the wilderness of the sea, like Faneesh had written down her memoirs as the waves of life smacked her around and changed the course of her life. God gave Pi an important sign when he found a human tooth on the island he reached. A sign to save himself, for the island gave its bounty during the day only to take it back at night, and God had given me the dream as a sign so that I would change.

Faneesh's eyes teared up. She told me it was the first time she'd ever entered a movie theater in her life. She didn't know how to thank me. I watched her reactions. Her newfound happiness. Her surprise at everything she saw or tasted for the first time. She laughed spontaneously. She told me stories that were not about cleaning or cooking, and when her energy for talking got going

HUDA HAMED

and her voice was liberated, I remembered what she had written in her journal, *"I resemble the slippers that I wear, and I fear forgetting my voice."*

We returned after the long outing. Pi and his journey with Richard Parker, the vicious tiger whom his father had forbidden him from approaching at the zoo, were on my mind. Pi had tamed the tiger in the wide sea. He tamed it in the midst of a predicament that limited his choices. Either he would domesticate him, or Richard Parker was going to gobble him up in a moment of blind hunger. I resemble you, Pi. I am taming the tigers of my thoughts so that they don't ravish me. I am taming the fragility of my soul. I am taming more worthy reasons to live.

TWEN**25** FIVE

AMER AND I lay together in bed. He kissed my hands, his eyes full of questions.

"I had a long day," he said. "I wrote a lot, and I'm pleased with myself."

My face was close to his, our breathing was calm.

"Amer, I've decided to draw Faneesh."

Amer was surprised.

"As a maid? A servant?"

I shook my head no.

"As I see her now."

Amer wrapped his arms around my waist and pulled me close to him. I felt his heartbeat quicken. I know this lap, I know this fetal curling up, this longing that doesn't heal. I pressed gently on his protruding vertebrae and sang to him a song that he loved. "*Oh how many people there were on the corner, waiting for others, and it would rain and they'd hold umbrellas. But even on the clearest days, no one would wait for me.*"

Amer slept, stuck to me as usual. I didn't move. I kept watching the ceiling, thoughts taking me right and left. A feeling of peace dwelled inside me, so I closed my eyes and slept.

HUDA HAMED